The Little Thing

The Little Thing

A Tale of Fairies

by

Roy Luna

TEN THOUSAND WORDS PRESS
MIAMI

SOL◡TION HOLE PRESS

First Edition
Second Printing: June, 2022

ISBN: 978-1-954267-03-9 hard cover (Cloth-Blue)
ISBN: 978-1-954267-04-6 soft cover (Perfect Bound)
ISBN: 978-1-954267-05-3 ebook

Ten Thousand Words Press
imprint of Solution Hole Press LLC.
www.solutionholepress.com

Cover Design: Six Penny Graphics
Cover Illustration: McKenzie Bunting
Author's picture courtesy of Mark P. Young

for Roxie Luna Muñoz

Preface:

The raison d'être of this story has to do with my little niece asking me one day, "Uncle Woy, have you ever written a book for children?" "Why, no," I answered, feeling woefully deficient in this serious omission on my part. Promptly, I asked her, "What would you like it to be about?" "Faiwies," was her answer. "Garden fairies?" I wanted to know, just to make sure. "Yes."

Thus was born *The Little Thing*, a book for children. The writer in me is enchanted by this foray into the realm of fairies, whom Icelanders call the Huldufólk. To explore their world, to be charmed by their peculiar habits, fascinated by their world views, and in complete agreement with their discontent over humanity's despoilment of the earth, is both an enthralling but simultaneously a disquieting romp. Fairies will allow a well-chosen few to frolic in their magical utopia, all the while letting the rest of mankind know that they are watching, judging, and condemning humans for the ruination of the planet and the enslavement of fellow creatures. In the midst of enchantment lies uneasiness.

However, the editor in me, who neither sits on my right ("straight") or left ("sinister") shoulder, quibbles about the choice of vocabulary within the pages of this book. "Quibble," for instance. Literary agents, editors at publication houses, reviewers and critics of books, all speak up in thunderous clamor. No modern kid is expected to know the word "quibble"! I agree with them all. No modern kid is expected to know the meaning of the word "quibble" because the expectations made on the modern American kid have been so diminished and the standards so abridged, that it is no wonder that the new norm has kids languishing at the bottom of the vocabulary barrel. Perish the thought that they go through the hardship of looking up words in a… gulp!… dictionary! Even when it is now easier to do so online! It is a thing of the past to lift up the heavy tome and riffle through its alphabetical pages. Now you can whisper the obtrusive word to your smart phone and get the full web treatment, from meaning to etymology to examples of its usage. In spite of modern tools, the intentional act of dumbing down books apparently makes them easier to sell.

Poor kids. "Like" is now their word of choice, peppering their language like stray interjections gone wild; like fillers trying in vain to fill up the holes in their lexicons; like truncated similes that come the closest to an approximation of what they want to say; like vain attempts to express themselves with precision, clarity, and discernment. Pity the modern American kid. Sent into adulthood with nary a modicum of vocabulary. Linguists will tell you: limit the words, limit the thoughts those words represent. Limiting the means with which to express the thoughts of the mind and the sentiments of the heart leads to hobbled lives of quiet desperation and of inarticulate frustration.

Do we really, like, want to quibble about this?

WEDNESDAY, APRIL 1ST, NIGHT

In the middle of the night, not too long ago, I woke up, as older people often do, chased awake by some random preoccupation or spurred by a peculiar ache or cramp. I could not go back to sleep. Not turning on a lamp, for I've read that throwing light on the retina reduces the chance of being able to fall back asleep right away, I headed to the bathroom to take care of another nuisance that besets the elderly man. While I was taking my piddle, out of my second-floor bathroom window I saw my garden, beautiful even in the dark, but suddenly I was startled to see the street beyond it lit up like an airport landing strip. It took only a second to realize that the source of the light must be the headlights of a car farther down the road. I wondered who, and for what reason, was driving so early in the morning. Perhaps it was a doctor on the way to her pre-dawn shift, or a voyager off to the airport to catch a red-eye. I felt happy to know I was not that poor soul compelled to curtail his sleep and leave his home at such an ungodly hour. I would soon be setting my head upon my warm pillow again. A second later, the car passed the house with a trail of blazing yellow headlights and red taillights along with a momentary burst of a wailing voice accompanied by musical instruments fluctuating to a climbing, then a descending, pitch. The road went dark and silent again.

It was just at this very moment that my eye caught a twinkling in the garden, almost as if the passing headlights had magically released some of their light in little sparkles that landed on the elephant ear like stranded fireflies. (The elephant ear, or *Colocasia gigantea,* is a native of South East Asia and grows a cluster of giant leaves about a meter across.) But we have no fireflies in Miami. We just have lightning bugs which usually don't swarm together, save for one moonless night a year when they go through their mating dance, but that was when we still had fields and meadows. Only an old man who has lived in South Florida for half a century can remember how it used to be in the time of fields and meadows when elevated highways didn't arc over our heads, when phalanxes of electric posts didn't buzz and crackle along the parallel cables they held up like the grungy green strands of hair from a giant troll, when strip malls and ghastly U-store-it buildings didn't dot the landscape from here to the horizon. I think the lightning bugs moved way out to the Everglades to do their mating dance, for I hadn't seen their twinkling, phantasmagoric dance in decades.

My eyes were still sharp enough to detect this small cluster of gleaming sparks shine and glitter for a few seconds after the car had passed, and I wondered as to its cause. I remember once, after a rain, seeing some similar twinkles in the garden in the dead of night, but the little lights did not move. The following morning when I went out to investigate, I observed a compact drop of water, a transparent pearl that, because of the physics of adhesion and cohesion, beaded up at the crux of stem and leaf among the giant leaves of the elephant ear. A magical drop of water caught at the base of each leaf reflected the sunlight in a dazzling luminosity of miniature proportion. I wondered if something similar were happening here tonight, only I realized that it hadn't rained. Nor had the sprinklers been on. Furthermore, these tiny lights had motion to them, even though a quick glance at the overhead canopy told that there was no breeze. The palm fronds were motionless, the oak branches stock-still. Not even the powder puffs, light as they were, showed the slightest shift. To my mind was recalled the erratic zigzag movement known as Brownian motion that is observed when particles are suspended in a medium. Only here, nothing was suspended, unless the particles were motes floating in the air. Stranger still, their movements did not seem erratic at all. What I was seeing from my bathroom window seemed to be movements guided by an intelligence, for the sparkles would travel together for a second, then split, then gather back, then move around each other, finally moving back in unison. It seemed to me as if the little lights were dancing, like brief interludes of square dancing, or line dancing, or better yet, waltzing in a 19th-century ballroom. But motes don't dance, and if they were insects, well, they only meet once, to mate, and then that's it, I think. Right? I had never seen fireflies coordinate their movements. Besides, we have no fireflies in South Florida.

As I watched the little gleams of light shimmer and flicker in the dark, they continued their magical motion for a few seconds more before they grew dim and went out. Curiosity beckoned to me, but so did my pillow. If I didn't try to go back to sleep I would certainly be sorry in the morning. I'd be cantankerous for the rest of the day. I promised myself to check out the natural phenomenon during the light of morning. Surely the cause of the twinkling little lights would be revealed under the sun and by the light of evidence and reason.

I went back to bed, and with the help of countless sheep and some lightning bugs thrown in, I managed to fall back asleep.

After percolating my morning coffee, and after feeding the hungry and demanding cats, I marched out, mug in one hand, progressive glasses in the other, to the front yard where I fully expected to lay my mind at ease and discover the reason for the mysterious twinkles I had observed in the middle of the night.

The beauty of the garden in the morning gladdened my heart and soothed my spirit. Under the tall oaks, birds chirped, butterflies flit, bees buzzed, all surrounded by the redolent waft of the ylang-ylang tree releasing its final burst of perfume before it fell asleep for the day. Soon, warmed by the sun, the gardenias would take over.

I identified monarchs and fritillaries and yellow sulphurs among the butterflies. Over the firebush, the coral honeysuckle and the jatropha, hummingbirds hovered to sip at their nectar. I sipped my coffee, enjoying their dance among the early-morning blooms. Their dance reminded me of the mysterious nocturnal twinkles, so I headed directly for the elephant ear. Each leaf was about a meter wide and a meter and a half long, with the leaf at the very center a little bigger than the rest. The silly thought came to me that the twinkling lights from last night, whatever they were, had been using the largest of the elephant leaves as if it were a stage or a dance floor, or perhaps, in contrast to the proportion to their diminutive size, an arena.

I put on my glasses and scrutinized the elephant leaves like Anton van Leeuwenhoek peering down his microscope to discover protozoa or Louis Pasteur squinting at yeast cells in fermentation. The leaves were quite dry, I noticed without surprise, since we were still in the middle of the dry season. There were no drops of water beaded up at the base of each leaf. No dew, no sap, no liquid residue of any kind. I put my forefinger on the largest leaf and it gave way under my touch. I felt along its veins, enjoying the coolness and smooth texture.

"Nice elephant," I said to it as I stroked it. "Good elephant."

Next to the elephant ear was a Mussaenda. Its cream-colored bracts also called out for my touch. Besides that there was an orange jasmine, still without flowers, but by rustling a few of its leaves, I was able to bring out a citrusy scent. My heart was content.

But still I thought as I glanced back at the elephant ear, what could I have seen last night? I knew it had not been a dream. There had to be some explanation for it. It could not have been the reflection of the moon for there had been no moon. Moreover, what would have reflected the moonlight? It could not have been starlight, either, for in Miami, unfortunately, there is no starlight to speak of. Very few stars are visible to us. We have to travel an hour into the Everglades before the glare of city lights diminishes. And even then the dome of light still remains visible to the east, like a fake rising sun or the aftermath of a nuclear explosion. I shook off this course of reasoning: the leaves of an elephant ear are not reflective. The moon could have been full, the Milky Way could have been in its full glory of shimmering across the heavens, but their light would not have bounced off the matte green of the leaves.

Besides, I had to keep telling myself, these twinkling little lights had been dancing. I chuckled to myself. The twinkling little lights were dancing? Right, and I was flying. A dark thought lurked in the shadows of my mind: I must have been hallucinating. Such a thought I refused to accept. Better to think that my eyes needed examining. I needed to make an appointment with the opthalmo–… the optal–… the ophthal–… with the eye doctor. I was seeing things. Clearly my vision was deceiving me. I decided with assurance that if there were a problem, it was truly with my retina, not my mind.

I closed my eyes. I could remember very well how those lights moved. They moved in tandem for a while, then they separated in symmetrical arcs, then they rejoined, this time perpendicularly, only to repeat the same entire pattern. Surely a natural phenomenon would not show such a pattern. There was choice here, in the movement of the little lights, also repetition, intention, volition. And if I were seeing things, why didn't I see any lights elsewhere?

Why only on this one spot? I walked back to the elephant ear. I smacked the biggest of the leaves with my open palm. It bowed down for a second before its thick stem brought it back up. Why only here, on this leaf, at the very center of this giant colocasia?

I looked up to my bathroom window on the second floor. It was a clear, straight, unimpeded view that I had of this staging area. I harrumphed like a failed alchemist unable to make gold. Still, I stood rooted to the spot. I stood deep in thought in front of the elephant ear and caressed it, wondering at the secrets it held.

"Nice elephant," I said. "Good elephant."

Rick in the Colocasia

Second Event:

Thursday, April 2, night

Well, suffice it to say that the next night I was ready for more observation from my upstairs window. The call of nature woke me up and, as I relieved myself leisurely, I glanced out the window in the direction of the elephant ear. I saw nothing. On this second night, there was a slight breeze for the boughs billowed in sluggish movement. Despite the wind rippling through the leaves of the trees and bushes, I saw no glint of light, no glimmer of luminescence. I viewed all the parts of the garden visible to me, but I espied nothing that emitted either twinkle or spark. I was disappointed but stood at the window long after my main task was done.

I was about to return to my bed when one of my neighbors from across the street turned on a light. Its gleam didn't shine very brightly, but it was enough to kindle a feeble pointillistic series of dots on the aforementioned central leaf of the elephant ear. My eyes pivoted immediately to it. Yes! The dots were moving! Just then, my neighbor's light was extinguished. No! Not yet! The dots took only seconds before they, too, went out.

Here was more scientific evidence! It was fluorescent light that was appearing on the leaf. The little dancing dots borrowed the light from some other source and played it forth. I quickly sprang to action. I ran to the HomeBrainiac panel in my bedroom and turned on the lights in the hallway downstairs. I ran back to the bathroom window and looked out to observe. The hallway lights threw shadows on the driveway, and a few shafts of light fell on the plants growing beyond it. I looked at the elephant ear. The sparkling, glimmering, dancing lights were back! They were not as luminous as when the car's headlights had lent them their brighter borrowed light, but they were strong enough that I was able to watch at length and observe their antics. Their movements were unmistakably deliberate. They moved to a rhythm. They were following some sort of cadence, like polka dots dancing to an inaudible tempo. I could not believe my eyes. My mind could not believe what it was thinking.

I turned off the lights downstairs. I rushed back to the window and saw that the little lights lasted for a few more seconds before they went dark. When I turned the hallway lights back on, the little lights sprang back.

My curiosity could bear it no longer. I rushed downstairs wearing only my underwear, grabbed the flashlight that I keep in the laundry room, and ran out of the house. I shone the beam of light right on the elephant leaf and saw… nothing. There was nothing there. No lights, no dots, no nothing. I turned the leaf up and peered underneath it. Nothing there, either. "What the…?" I thought. I looked at the other leaves. I looked at the other plants. I looked up at the oak branches, down at the ground, across the driveway to the wall of the house, up into the sky. I whirled around everywhere, looking for the dancing lights, thinking of insects, owls and night jars and other nocturnal birds, large fluorescent moths, thinking of natural phenomena, of bioluminescent creatures of the sea, of weird animals and flying lights and dancing stars, of chemical emissions of light and heat lightning and St. Elmo's fire with luminous plasma and laser light streaming in the skies, of *ignis fatuus* and will o' the wisps with their ghostly lights over bogs, swamps and marshes, mischievous pixie lights, of sparks from flint, shooting stars, falling meteors, plunging debris of space junk. My mind was overwhelmed, and my scientific training found it hard to grasp that I had observed points of light dancing on a leaf. Points of light were not supposed to dance on a leaf, or any other place. Dancing was not allowed to inexplicable points of light.

In my temporary discomfiture, I dropped my flashlight and its beam shone crazily through the stems along the ground. I thought I saw a snail but when I looked closer it had disappeared. I was frustrated beyond endurance. I took the elephant leaf in my hands and shook it, but it remained smooth and dark and impassive, although the light of the flashlight beneath it penetrated parts of it translucently. I wanted to shred the leaf with my hands, but I realized that my exasperation had nothing to do with the innocent leaf. I released it, gathered my flashlight and went inside. I turned off all the lights. I didn't go upstairs to my bedroom but stayed in the media room, there to sort through my thoughts and try to make sense of my observations. I was well aware that humankind didn't know all of the answers about the universe surrounding us, but things that move with conviction here on earth were pretty much accounted for. What I had seen, two nights in a row, was inexplicable, and I felt angry and ashamed to be unable to find an answer for it.

Assailed by dark thoughts, I must have fallen asleep, for I woke up in the morning on the sofa, with the TV on in front of me, but without the memory of having turned it on. The remote was not close by, I noticed. It was still in its cradle across the room.

Third event:

Wednesday, April 8, day

A week later I was still feeling quite miserable. I had scoured the internet looking for possible explanations to the natural phenomena I had observed. I found only references to elves, leprechauns, fairies, Icelandic Huldufólk, extraterrestrial beings, and telekinetic pranksters. I followed threads of chats, but did not participate, about strange flashes of light people had seen inside their homes. Others spoke about strange changes of temperature or air pressure when their ears popped. Many spoke of TVs turning on or off by themselves. "Aha!" I said to myself. But I couldn't quite believe the causes cited by the web pages: spirits, ghosts, poltergeists, and similar creatures abounded in the internet. The internet, I found once again, was chock-full of the most outlandish, absolutely unscientific material, and it was not to be trusted. The internet, it is true, is the world's vast depository of human knowledge, wisdom and folly, but the minds of most people are still as irrational as when we skulked around as troglodytes spooked by our own shadows.

Nowhere, however, did I find even one reference to twinkling lights moving in symmetry in a garden. In the sky, yes, big lights moving fast this way and that across the heavens, but not small ones moving on a big leaf. Perhaps I had pygmy UFOs cavorting on my colocasia leaves.

Naturally, I told no one about my experience. My family is pretty scientifically minded, and we tend not to go to church. I believe I'm the only atheist in the family, but a sister who used to go to church does so no longer, another had her child baptized "just in case," and my brother and I have never broached the subject of the supernatural and miracles and saintly apparitions. My friends are also mostly the kind that are tethered to reality. Only one of my friends, Joan-Agnes, in truth a very close friend, believes in ghosts and is certain that she has seen them, or at least heard them, walking across the room, a couple of times. I pride myself in having an open mind, and I welcome any ghost to come visit me, but so far, not one has taken me up on my invitation.

I've been tempted to tell Joan-Agnes about my lights, but each time I talk to her, I lose my nerve. I've also lost my courage about repeating the experiment. Now when I use the bathroom in the middle of the night, I look straight ahead of me at the wall where I have a picture of a Grecian shepherd, Pan flute in one hand, the other shading his eyes as he looks at the horizon. And I turn on the bathroom light so it darkens the view out the window.

Am I afraid? Does the occurrence of lights dancing on a leaf fill me with dread? Does it make me think that I'm losing it? Am I terrified to think that my sanity is straying? Just in case, I've made an appointment with an ophthalmologist. I haven't had my eyes checked in a couple of years anyway, so it was due.

In the meantime, I avoided the front garden even during the day. But after about a week, I gravitated back to it in order to prune the Mussaenda, fertilize the orchids, and do some general weeding. The elephant ear looked imposing, as it generally does because of its large size, but it certainly wasn't sinister. It just looks like an oversized prehistoric piece of vegetation, quite in proportion with huge dinosaurs roaming about, its leaves big enough to hide the teeny scurrying mammals that were eventually to take over.

Why didn't I just remain in the back yard?

Just on cue, as I approached the elephant ear, I saw something scurry beneath its mammoth leaves and hide in the leaf litter. Lizard, I thought. We have so many lizards in South Florida that, in spite of the myriad species of animals that feast on them—ibises, little blue herons, kingfishers, red-shoulder hawks, kestrels, morning owls, raccoons, corn snakes, domestic cats and dogs, and even my chickens!—the predators don't make much of a dent in their population.

The creature I thought was a lizard kept burrowing into the mulch surrounding the stems of the plants. I thought then it must be a rodent. Now, mice and rats may be cute to some people, but I've never held a place close to my heart for them. With my bare foot I followed the movement, upturning the mulch with my big toe in the attempt to uncover the creature. To my surprise, the little thing took wing and fled from danger. It happened so fast, and I was so startled, that I was not able to recognize the species of bird. But then I chided myself. What kind of bird hides, and burrows, through leaf litter?

I knew that catbirds, of which a pair hang out in my backyard by the garden shed, search through litter to garner bugs and such, but I've never heard of them burrowing in it. I couldn't even say what color the bird was. I think it was mostly a mousy brown, but perhaps I saw a blur of blue on the wings, maybe some yellow? It happened so quickly, I couldn't tell. Now I can't remember.

I was disappointed in myself. I should be a better observer of nature. Later, when I was back inside the house, I called my friend James Skutch at the Audubon Society and asked him what type of birds hid, or rather burrowed, in leaf litter. He answered immediately that he didn't know of any, but that there were plenty that gleaned for prey in the litter. He started enumerating them as if he were reading from a book, but I knew he wasn't.

"Rufous scrub-bird, woodcrawler, eastern whipbird, white-throated rock thrush, grey catbird, grey wagtail, warblers, woodcocks, juncos…"

I had to interrupt him. "What about birds that actually plunge into the litter to hide?"

"Birds with working wings take to the air to escape from predators. Flightless birds run away as fast as they can. Those that don't, well, end up like the dodo."

"Jim," I told him, "I just saw a bird burrow through the leaf litter like a rodent. When I tried to uncover it, that's when it took flight."

There was silence on the other end of the line. "Jim, are you there?" I asked after a few seconds.

"Yeah, I'm still here. I'm trying to think about what you saw, or think you saw. You don't think that perhaps there was a bird nesting on the litter? You know, they camouflage themselves rather well, those types of birds. Quail, partridges, whip-poor-wills, ruffed grouse, ovenbirds—"

"We don't even have ovenbirds in South Florida, Jim! What are you talking about?"

"I'm talking about birds that nest on the ground and fly straight up when you flush them out. They jump up like they're on springs. And yes, we do have ovenbirds in South Florida. We're part of their wintering range."

"Well, this bird did not jump up like on a spring; it flew sideways under an elephant ear I have in the front yard. And before that, it had been burrowing in the leaf litter like a mouse. I could hear it crackle through the dry leaves."

Then I remembered the ovenbird. "And if it was indeed an ovenbird, it's late leaving its wintering range, and besides, it would not be nesting here."

Jim tried to be diplomatic. "Well, don't ruffle your feathers! I'm just trying to think of what you saw. Perhaps it was a burrowing owl, you think, maybe?"

"You know very well burrowing owls need to have a burrow. There is no burrow underneath my elephant ear. This thing, whatever it was, had been burrowing in the litter, not hiding in a burrow!"

Jim made a few noises and several attempts to speak, but I knew he was stumped.

"Well, call me back, Jim, once you have a better idea. I know what I saw, and I know what I heard. I heard the little thing moving through the leaf litter. I could see the disturbance of the leaf litter as the thing moved through it, and when I moved the litter back with my toe, I saw the creature fly away, not straight up like quails, but sideways, like… like… like all other birds. Except flightless ones, of course."

"Do you remember its color?"

Now I was embarrassed that my observational skills left a lot to be desired.

"I think it was brown, with some blue, maybe some yellow."

"Brown, blue and yellow? Brown, blue and yellow?" Jim repeated with increasing volume and, frankly, incredulity.

"Yes," I reiterated. "Brown… yellow… blue. Not much yellow, I think."

"The male eastern bluebird has blue wings, so does the bluewinged pitta. But the bluebird comes south as far as Orlando, and the pitta lives in Australia and Southeast Asia."

"So there we have it. I saw an impossible bird. The bird I saw this morning, in the leaf litter under my elephant ear, is impossible! It does not exist!"

After a momentary hesitation, Jim asked cautiously, "Do you think it might have been some sort of insect?"

"Jim, thanks for your time, but I need to get back to my life. I'll call you later, okay?"

And with that, I hung up the phone. Jim and I have been friends for such a long time, but sometimes he irks me with his encyclopedic knowledge of the natural world.

Thursday, April 9, day

Frustration gave birth to enterprise and ingenuity.

I already had indoor cameras inside the house connected to a security system. I went out and bought a bunch of exterior cameras and set them up around and above the elephant ear. I also bought two 1,200-watt halogen tripod work lights. I figured these would shine lots of light directly on the subject. I ran three extension cords from the garage out to the front garden, secured the cameras from the branches of neighboring trees, fixed and focused them on the central elephant leaf, went inside to my computer and set up the new security area which I called "Front Garden."

The system looked good. Everything was sharply in focus. I could see beyond the elephant ear in all directions to a radius of about thirty feet, with the central staging area right in the middle. I was again glad nobody could read my thoughts. Central staging area. Central staging area for what? For dancing lights? For strange night creatures? For elusive impossible flying rodents? For little elves and sprites? What was I doing?

I knew what I was doing. I grew up and lived during a time that, when faced with a conundrum, you did something about it. You used the old noggin, you figured things out, you set up your investigative experiment, then you waited to observe, calculate, analyze, extrapolate, everything you had to do in order to procure your findings. We are a can-do society, a self-reliant generation, and I was not going to let myself be defeated by the weird, the rare, or the unimaginable. If anything, I told myself, I would find out if my eyes were defective. Eyes can deceive; senses can run amok. I realized now that the headlights of a passing car and the lightbulbs of a distant hallway were insufficient. These mega lights from the hardware store would light up the front garden like an airport runway, and the cameras would be recording every leaf that stirred and snail that crawled. I could hardly wait for evening.

By the way, the cameras also recorded audio, so if there was any music to accompany the dancing lights, that detail would become part of the proceedings. I meant to get an air-tight case, or yield to the likelihood that I needed my eyes checked or my mind examined. "Music to accompany the dancing lights," indeed. I would be the first to admit I was loony.

My computer was ready. There were six views from different angles on the screen, three of the general area, but three zoomed in to the dance hall ground zero. The last items I arranged on my library table were a canister of mixed nuts, a few chocolate energy bars, and a bag of gluten-free multi-grained crackers. The coffee I would brew at the last minute.

Then I went off to an afternoon nap. I figured it might be a long night. I needed to stockpile energy to be awake and alert for a possible drawn-out vigil.

THURSDAY, APRIL 9, EVENING, TO FRIDAY, APRIL 10, DAWN

My alarm rang at 6 in the evening. Sundown wasn't for another hour but I wanted to be ready. I went down to the garden to make sure all the equipment remained undisturbed. Everything looked satisfactory. Before going back up, I turned on the klieg lights that made that front part of the garden look like a movie set. The garden never looked so beautiful. It was ready for its close-up.

The sun sank towards the horizon, lengthening the shadows and casting a beautiful pink and peach hue to the western sky. The front of the house faces east, so the front garden is always first to be plunged into darkness. But the heavy-duty lamps illuminated the area of the elephant ear so you could see every single vein.

The birds made their last calls of the day, and a few crickets began their first tentative chirps. A tree frog, probably soaking inside a bromeliad, gave a few croaks, then became silent. The screech owl began its melancholy trilling. Every once in a while, I could hear a car go past, but no headlights registered on the scene since the lamps were so bright.

I knew I would have to go downstairs eventually and unplug the lamps. The little twinkles became visible only when the lights went out. Or perhaps their twinkles were in proportion so weak that they were visible only in the darkness, and then only after a source of light had given them the ability to fluoresce. I was hoping that the intense light of the lamps would increase their fluorescence and perhaps make it last longer.

My patience gave out before midnight. At 11:30 I went downstairs to the laundry room and unplugged the kliegs. I ran back upstairs, two steps at a time.

When I saw the screen of my computer, my heart leapt. As I expected, all was in darkness, save for the dance floor. As I hoped, there were twinkling little lights in the frame of all six cameras, dots of light that were moving, all centered on the biggest leaf of the elephant ear.

I made sure that the cameras were recording. I increased the volume and slowly began to hear little clicking noises. It certainly didn't sound like music, but I determined that the clicks had a rhythm, and that the movement of the little lights were synchronized with the clicks. I increased the volume a little more. The clicks were not just percussion, I discovered. Some of them lingered, some of them were staccato, a few sounded as if they changed pitch. Astounding!

I could not believe my ears. I was now distrusting my ears the way I had distrusted my eyes. But how could I deny what was on the split screens? Six—six!—images that confirmed my earlier observations. I stared at them completely transfixed and unable to move. I heard my heart pounding wildly inside my chest. The hand that held the mouse trembled. I was having some sort of experience, when ordinary science doesn't go far enough, when one is treading on new ground, unable to identify a new phenomenon but quite capable of recognizing its importance. I was seeing and hearing something phenomenal, but what it was, I had no idea! All I could see were the little dancing lights, and I could now confirm that the movement was circular at the outside, delineating the diameter of a circle that went almost to the edges of the elephant leaf, but that involved parallel and perpendicular lines on the inside, and arcs of at least 90°. It was geometric, in a sense, for the little lights moved in factors of 2, i.e., 2, 4 and 6, and they moved in pairs always staying within the circle. If this were a square dance, it was very convoluted indeed.

Bees make similar dances when they return to the hive and communicate information about the distance and direction of food. But the bee's dance is in isolation. Her sister bees congregate around her and as each of them learns the particulars of the coordinates of the food, they fly away. Here, all the little lights remained consistent. No new ones joined in, as far as I could tell, and of the ones already there, not a one seemed to leave.

The little lights remained visible for about half an hour. I had been right in surmising that the strong lamps would fortify the little dots, in intensity and in duration. When everything on the leaf went dark, I ran downstairs and turned the lamps on again. I waited ten minutes, then turned them off. Up at the computer, the twinkles lasted for about a minute. When I next turned on the lamps, I kept them on for twenty minutes. The twinkles lasted for two minutes. In this way, I was able to ascertain that for every ten minutes of artificial light, the twinkles "borrowed" the light for a minute. For the last experiment of the night, I left the lamps on for two hours. The twinkles shone while they danced for a little over a quarter of an hour.

Then the light of dawn started to creep up from the east. I turned on the lamps one last time, for ten minutes, then shut them off, but the little dots did not reappear. The elephant leaf remained deserted and quiet. The arrival of the sun put an end to the square dance.

Exhausted, I turned away from the computer and contemplated going to bed for a few hours. As I walked to my bedroom, however, my mind was working a mile a minute.

There were a few things I could say with accuracy.

No matter the movement of the little dots, the leaf did not budge, save for occasional fluttering by a breeze. In other words, I doubted that the twinkles had sufficient weight to move the leaf. I was going to have to experiment with the leaf to see the minimum weight required to make it bend down.

The little dots knew geometry. Besides the outside ring, a circle, they also knew how to describe isosceles triangles, pie-shaped, made up of the circle's radii. They formed arcs along parts of the diameter of the circle. They marched along the outlines of parallelograms, including diamonds and rhombi. I looked forward to analyzing their movements, but I already knew that the little buggers knew their math.

I could say pretty safely that the dots did not emit their own light. Time and time again, they had lost the intensity of their brightness little by little until they grew dim and then went completely out. They did indeed appropriate their luminosity from other sources, and the duration of their radiance was in direct proportion to the intensity and duration of the source.

The clicks, long and short as they were, staccato or legato, were a complete mystery to me. How they were emitted was impossible to ascertain. Crickets will rub body parts together to create their chirps. What did the little dots have to do to create their clicks? Friction would mean that they had body parts. But other than the light they emitted, I could see no other evidence of their existence. If they indeed had little bodies, they were so light that a whole group of them, a ballroom-size of them, was unable to make the leaf itself dance up and down to the rhythm. What an enigma! How would I be able to conjure up an explanation for that one?

How would I be able to conjure up a satisfactory, rational, *scientific* explanation for what the little twinkles were? I had proof now, evidence that I was not crazy. It was there for anyone to see, on the computer. Still, I was reluctant to share it with anybody just yet. I needed more time to think. Analysis takes time, it takes patience. Good science is not built in a day. It needs to be pursued, cultivated, developed, refined. It needs calibration, elbow grease, and, above all, persistence. I believe I could come up with all that, but for the moment, my brain was so very tired, all I could think of was my pillow. My soft, fluffy, goose-down pillow drew me like a magnet. I think I was asleep before my head even touched it.

Friday, April 10, noon

I woke up late. I couldn't believe it was already noon.

I saw the lights were on in my bedroom. The lights were on in the upstairs hallway and in the staircase going down. The lights were also on in the kitchen. They seemed to be blazing all over the house. I went to the HomeBrainiac screen in the kitchen and turned them all off. How could I have been so careless last night? Yet, I was puzzled because I never turn on all the lights of the house at the same time. I abhor waste.

Without lingering in the kitchen for my usual coffee and meditation, I threw down some food for the cats whose emphatic meows indicated their annoyance at being fed so late. I immediately ran outside. The day was sunny and bright, and the humidity of summer, I could tell, was well on its way with its thuggish agenda.

I examined the stage set, found nothing to be amiss, and with an index finger I touched the central elephant ear leaf, the locus of all the nocturnal hoopla I had recorded during the night. With the slightest touch, the whole leaf, all one meter by a meter and a half of it, would sway, then spring back up when I removed my finger. Boy, those little lights must not have much weight at all, for a whole ballroom of them could not sway the leaf one iota!

Out of the corner of my eye I saw a flurry of movement. I turned in time to see a bird fly into a cavity of a nearby oak. I remembered that cavity: a limb had succumbed to the winds of hurricane Wilma a few years ago, and the tree had grown new bark around it but not enough to plug up the hole. Intrigued, I silently walked up to it. I was curious because I knew of no bird who would want to nest in a hole so close to the ground, about a meter and a half, which would leave it in danger from predators, especially snakes, and, frankly, me.

Without thinking much about it, I placed my open palm on the cavity. My hand wasn't nearly big enough to cover it, so I brought my other hand to help block it off. Just in that instant, I felt something hit the palm of my hand which automatically closed on it. Whatever it was felt soft and smooth and it immediately began to wriggle in an attempt to escape. The movements of what I supposed were its legs tickled my palm.

My heart gave a leap of exhilaration and alarm to feel the little body squirming in my hand. I thought I had caught a bird, but the feel of the feathers just wasn't quite right. Feathers feel soft, to be sure, but dry to the touch, and you detect, or at least think you detect, the individual barbs as they start to break apart on your skin. After all, it's to realign these barbs that birds spend so much time preening. But when you hold a bird, bits of feather will often stick to your skin, and if the bird is beating its wings, feather fluff will fly out in all directions.

This wasn't happening with the little creature that had flown up into my hand. As I held on to it, I expanded my thumb and forefinger a smidgeon to be able to peer inside. No fluff flew out, nothing stuck to my hand. As a matter of fact, as I observed this little beast as it struggled to escape my grasp, I could not identify any feathers at all. Its little body felt very soft, that was beyond question, but it wasn't dry. It wasn't moist, either. It was silky smooth, cool to the touch, perhaps akin to reptilian scales, only without the scales. As I stared down at the little thing agitating its body and trying to flap its wings in a courageous attempt to free itself, I was startled by my observations: there was no beak at the end of its little head; it emitted cries that sounded like no bird I've ever heard; and I could detect expressions, yes, expressions, on its little face, expressions that I could recognize! The little rounded face, with big lips that reminded me of those on a fish, showed distress, fear, sadness, despair. Its calls were sighing moans interspersed with clicks and weird guttural gulps, short little wails that seemed to be composed of both vowels and consonants. To all intents and purposes, it sounded like language. I was amazed and enthralled, riveted to the spot next to the oak tree. My heart raced with the acknowledgment that I held in my hand a creature unknown to all the nature books and documentaries I had ever read or seen. I couldn't even identify the little thing among the numerous phyla, orders, genera, and species of taxonomic classification that I had ever read about, to say nothing of what I had myself encountered in nature, and I've traveled the world to see animals in their natural habitats, from tropical jungles to deserts to tundra.

Here, I was stymied. This was no bird, no reptile, no amphibian, no flying fish, no insect, no known animal of any kind. My fist trembled as the little beast tried dauntingly to escape. In my shock of disbelief, I didn't want to crush it, so my other hand came up to the little head in an attempt to still its frenetic movements and to quiet its unnerving calls, or rather, utterances.

Immediately, other similar utterances arose all around me. I looked about but could see nothing. Still, I knew that I was surrounded by other creatures, but their existence was evidenced solely by observations of the ear. They were invisible to my eye. Were these creatures hiding? Perhaps camouflaged? Were they transparent? Were they even there? My ears told me that they were, for the chorus of calls became louder and more insistent, full of bickering and fright, a frenzy of sounds louder than crickets in a field or spring peepers in a pond. I was reminded of Pan, the god of the wilderness who, when disturbed by the intrusion of men, lets out cries that prompts all the creatures of the wild to emit their own calls of panic and pandemonium. I felt overwhelmed by the cries, disoriented by the brouhaha. But I considered it impossible to let go of the little mysterious creature, at least not until I had identified it. But how was I to identify this weird little thing trembling in my hand? I certainly didn't want to make it suffer, but the call of science was too strong. If I were holding a new species unknown to the annals of zoology, then it was my responsibility to bring it to light. But first I had to isolate it, and isolate myself from the growing chorus, in order to observe the creature in peace and quiet.

I fled the garden and ran into the house, shutting the door against the bickering vociferations of invisible creatures. I ran up the stairs into my library, hurried to the table where I have a trio of glass cloches, opened the closest one and knocked away its resident plant. Carefully thrusting my fist under the cloche, I released my quarry into it and immediately brought the glass cover down. The little thing landed in a heap on the glass floor inside the ring of stain left from the evicted potted plant. It landed there and did not move. I peered at it more closely. It looked dead. I suddenly felt an overwhelming sense of remorse. Had I killed it? Did my fist crush the very life out of the little being? I was distraught. I felt guilty for having ended the life of a little, sentient being. I stared at the little thing, wondering if I could do anything to revive it, to resuscitate it. How could I give CPR to a thing the size of a hummingbird?

C. LINNÆ
SYSTEMA
NATURÆ

I took out my magnifying glass the better to observe. Very slightly, the sides of its abdomen under its folded wings moved rhythmically in and out, like a lizard's does. I breathed a sigh of relief. It was alive. But why didn't it move? Maybe it had fainted. The sunlight from the window wasn't enough for me to see well, so I turned on my table lamp and brought it closer to the cloche. It lit up the little creature well enough for me to see its coloring.

It was quite colorful: a blue head, a yellow upper back, red-orange lower back, a green border in-between, and its wings and tail were a grayish purple with blue accents. Its upper breast was a neon red, more muted underneath. Since it had no feathers, the wings looked more like bat wings, only they didn't have the arm bones and scary looking claws that bats have. This is when I discovered, as wonderful and improbable as it was, that the little being had little arms tucked under its wings. At the end of its arms I observed the tiniest of fingers. It looked like it had an opposable thumb. When I followed the contours of its body, I saw that its tail was no tail at all, but two quite distinct legs pressed together. Ornithologists will immediately recognize the species of bird this creature was mimicking: the painted bunting (Passerina ciris).

But the fantastic, out of this world discoveries were not yet over. As I watched, with the lamp right beside me shining down on the cloche (I could feel its warmth), the little thing began to glow. It started first on its back, between its wings, then traveled down and around its miniature body, and up to its little head. Before long, the pretty little thing was glowing like a— like a— what, what could I compare it to? I had never seen anything like it! The closest thing that I could compare it to was a star, for it shimmered, its skin fluttered in its colors, if I may put it that way. It indeed twinkled, and all my initial observations now appeared to have been true.

Here was a new species, one that contradicted all the corollaries of evolution, for it had both arms and wings, and it did not fit the characteristics of any known phylum, let alone genus or species. I couldn't even tell if it came from Mammalia, Aves, Reptilia or Amphibia. Could it have come from some weird class of Insecta, or perhaps even Arachnida, one whose first pair of legs had evolved into arms, its second pair into wings, its third pair into a second set of arms, and its fourth into legs? I didn't think so. It did not seem to have an exoskeleton. The only thing I could be sure of was that it most definitely was part of the phylum

Chordata, animals with a backbone. But what kind of terrestrial animals were bioluminescent? I had read of a fluorescent tree frog, the polka dot tree frog of South America. Maybe this little thing under the cloche was a type of frog, albeit a flying, glowing, iridescent frog. With three pairs of limbs and one pair of wings.

I saw movement. The little thing had budged. It moved its two little arms and used them to support its torso. I held my breath. It moved its little head up and around to observe its surroundings. When its gaze turned to me, it became startled and it lifted its head to see me, a giant, looming over it. In a panic it scrambled to its feet and was upright. It slowly backed away from me until it hit the back side of the cloche. It looked all around it and realized it was trapped. It sank to its little knees, as if in despair, and took an attitude of hopelessness and misery.

I was mesmerized. I found that I had been holding my breath and let out a deep sigh. Yet, in spite of my astonishment, I realized immediately that I was guilty of anthropomorphism: I was attributing human characteristics and human behavior to the little thing. This little thing, as sentient and intelligent in its own way as it might have been, certainly didn't, couldn't, have feelings the way humans do. Could it? Feelings are human. I mean, animals feel fright, they feel contentment, they feel loyalty. Elephants feel grief. But I never saw any of my three cats, no matter how much into a funk they had descended, sink to their knees in despondency. I've had dogs in my life before, but I never knew them to become as dispirited as this little creature seemed to be.

But it sure looked to me as if it were sad. All the gestures were there: body slumped, head down, hands dragging on the floor of the cloche's saucer. Hands. Hands! It had hands! I took my magnifying glass again and observed the creature's hands. Yes, I was right. Those were fingers! I counted them: a total of four, three fingers and a thumb. An opposable thumb. God in heaven! I thought only primates had opposable thumbs, chimpanzees, bonobos, orangutans, gorillas and gibbons. Outside of the order of primates, koalas, pandas, and possums also had them. all of them mammals. But so did this little thing. And it was more of an insect than anything else. A bird insect. A frog bird.

What kind of freaky evolution had gone on here? This creature showed signs of being an inter-class, perhaps an inter-phylum cross, a kind of missing link to a lot of evolutionary chains! I mean, when the platypus was first taken to England, it was thought to be a hoax. Zoologists thought that someone had sewn the beak and four webbed feet of two ducks and the tail of a beaver to a medium-sized marsupial mammal. Then the improbable animal laid an egg! It was more comfortable in the water than on land, like an amphibian; it had a venomous sting, like a reptile, and could detect weak electrical signals with its duckbill, like a… like a… like an ammeter.

When the dodo was first discovered, its murderers were stymied. It was definitely a bird, although completely flightless, and it had no fear of the humans who first encountered it. It would sidle up to them like a puppy dog. It was extinct in less than a century.

The axolotl, known as the Mexican walking fish, is no fish at all. It's a salamander, and thus an amphibian, with exterior gills that they never lose, as typical salamanders do when they go through metamorphosis. Their lidless eyes on their broad heads stare unblinkingly under the water. Extensively studied, their ability to regenerate whole limbs is well known. Unfortunately, they, too, are near extinction.

I had succeeded in making myself feel better. See? Strange animals do exist, so this little creature under my cloche was not alone in its strangeness. It just had to be analyzed and… and…

It had raised its head a bit and I thought I saw… I thought I saw… I raised my magnifying glass again and verified… Tears! The little thing was weeping!

I was about to start weeping myself! I felt I was going to burst. I needed to tell someone about this. I could no longer be all by myself with this mystery. I was about to go mad, berserk, absolutely bonkers!

Just then, I heard the garage door downstairs slam shut. It startled me. Then I realized it must be Luna returning home from her Spring Break in Key West.

I went down the stairs slowly, mulling over what I was going to tell my niece and how I was going to tell her. She and I had a close relationship and we shared everything in our lives. For a fleeting moment I considered keeping my weird discovery from her. After all, I never told her about the dancing lights I saw outside my window in the middle of the night. How could I when I scarcely believed what my own eyes thought they saw? I knew, however, that there was no way I was going to shut her out of this latest incident, as extraordinary as it could be, even though I had no idea how she was going to react to it. Would she react with consternation or with scoffing? Would she think her uncle had finally become unhinged? It would not take much to convince me that this was true.

I didn't find her in the kitchen which is the first place she goes to when she comes home from school. Like me, she doesn't have breakfast, and by lunchtime she's ravenous. She wasn't in the media room, either. I tried the dining room, living room and music room in quick succession, but she was nowhere to be seen. Maybe she had gone back to her car in the garage. On the way there, I saw her through the hallway windows. She was standing in front of the elephant ear plant, staring at all the cameras and klieg lights.

FRIDAY, APRIL 10, APPROXIMATELY 2 PM

I went out through the wine room door.

"What's all this?" Luna asked. "I saw it on my way in. Another of your experiments?"

A bit disconcerted, I answered with a quick, "Sorta."

It seems she followed the angle of all the cameras because she lay a gentle hand on the elephant ear. "I've always loved these. They remind me of the tropical rain jungle."

"Is it teatime?" I asked.

"Bit early, but why not?" she replied.

Ever since she was a little girl we've been having tea together, even when at first it was only make-believe. Luna would bring her dolls and stuffed toys, whom she called "my kids," and we all sat on the rug in the reading room around a red gingham picnic cloth to enjoy our tea. Luna and I are the only tea drinkers in the family. It's one of our little rituals that differentiates us from the rest.

"How was Spring Break?"

Luna gave me the three-minute version of her vacation in Key West, the highlight of which had been an impromptu beach party to celebrate the sunset, with dancing and a haphazard multinational collection of musicians providing the music.

"It was so cool! There were people there from all over the world. It's like we all got together at this one place to celebrate the earth, but also to celebrate our humanity, to move in a rhythm that united us all, under the rays of the setting sun, then under the starry sky, with the sea, dark, mysterious and boundless in front of us."

Luna could be quite lyrical at times. One of her favorite places on earth is the steps in front of the Basilica of Sacré-Cœur on top of Montmartre, at sunset, when a varied and eclectic crowd gathers to sing songs by the Beatles. I agree with her. It's magic, with all of Paris at our feet, singing a cappella or with the accompaniment of instrumentalists who join in. For an hour one can imagine that humanity can indeed come together, without the help of anyone, and feel that all we need is love, and that we're just fools on the hill as we sing all together and follow the sun as it slips beneath the curvature of the earth.

But Luna had more pressing matters to discuss.

"So what's with the experiment in the front yard?"

As our water boiled and I prepared the tea bags, I tried to think of how best to broach the subject of the little thing.

"I have been observing strange nocturnal activity outside," I ventured.

"Oh?" Luna said. I could tell already that her curiosity was on full alert. "With the neighbors?"

"No, no, not that…" I took a full breath. "Since last week there have been weird lights appearing in the front garden."

As she brought two cups down from the cupboard she turned to face me, her almond-shaped, chocolate-brown eyes looking directly into mine, her beautiful long brown hair bouncing in ringlets along her back.

"Click beetles?"

Luna was using another name for lightning bugs. Some people even called them devil bugs, for the two eyespots on their back where their bioluminescence comes from. As they fly through the air and those two "eyes" seem to be coming straight at you, well, some people find that sinister.

"Oh, yes. Click beetles. Some people do call lightning bugs by that name."

"Well, when they're turned on their back, they click their abdomen and jump into the air either to land upright or to fly away in case of danger. Very ingenious."

I took out the sugar, raw brown sugar in cubes, heavy cream, and sugar pincers and placed them on the table.

"I've always thought of those beetles as being so smart," she continued. "*Pyrophorus luminosus. Pyro* for 'fire,' *phorus,* as in *phosphorus,* for 'bring,' giving *pyrophorus* the meaning of 'bringer of fire,' since the ancients thought that it was a substance that ignited upon exposure to air. Now we know, of course, that bioluminescence is a chemical process."

Luna's knowledge of bugs always amused me. When she was but a little child she was intrigued by crawly things in the garden. She would even handle earthworms when we had to move them to another spot. Then in her pre-teens, due, I think, to the influence of other little girls, the idea of the "yuck" factor emerged. But later in high school, she became interested again. Now in university, one of her electives was entomology, and in particular, she was interested in insect metamorphosis. All the natural world became her oyster. She also became a militant naturalist, environmentalist, and climatologist. And she was only nineteen! I prided myself in having had some influence in her education.

I poured the hot water into the teacups. Luna dropped three sugar cubes into her tea and quite a bit of cream.

"No, these aren't *Pyrophorus luminosus* that I've been seeing. I don't think they are bugs at all. They… uhm… I've seen… them, ah, dancing… on a leaf. An elephant-ear leaf, to be exact."

Luna scrunched up her beautiful face as she took a sip of her tea. I knew it wasn't because of the tea. She loved English Breakfast.

"Dancing?" she asked. "You said you've seen them dancing?"

Was that a smile I saw forming on her lips, then quickly suppressed?

"That's right," I answered.

"And you said you've seen them dancing on a leaf?"

She looked up at the ceiling but I knew she was looking inwardly, at the information she kept in her head.

"Why would bugs limit their motion to a leaf?" she continued. "A single leaf?"

"That's why I don't think they're bugs. Yes, the biggest leaf of them all, the central one. The one you were just touching." I held my breath, then said, "They use it as if it were a stage."

"And why do you use the word dancing to describe the motion? Why not wriggling or squirming or wobbling?"

"Well, bees dance."

"You mean they waggle. It's a vibrating motion, probably accompanied by pheromone release, to tell the other bees about the location of food sources. It takes into consideration the position of the sun and the position of the food source. I wouldn't call it dancing."

"Well, you know, people do. When they don't understand exactly what is going on. I mean, what would extraterrestrial aliens think of humans waltzing in a ballroom?"

"They would call it spinning and rotating of a large flock of specimens. A sort of human murmuration."

I chuckled. "Like starlings. I suppose you're right." After some thought, I added, "All right. They weren't dancing. These spots of light were delineating geometrical patterns on the surface of a big leaf."

It was Luna's turn to chuckle. "Uncle Rick, are you mad? You're making this up. April Fools was last week."

My look must have convinced her that I was not kidding, faking, or duping.

"Is that what all that equipment is doing outside?"

"That's right."

In a couple of minutes I described to her my nocturnal experiment and my conclusions about the contagious luminescence of the little lights. I took a notepad, a pencil and a pair of eyeglasses that I keep on all the tables of the house and drew her a diagram. It looked like this:

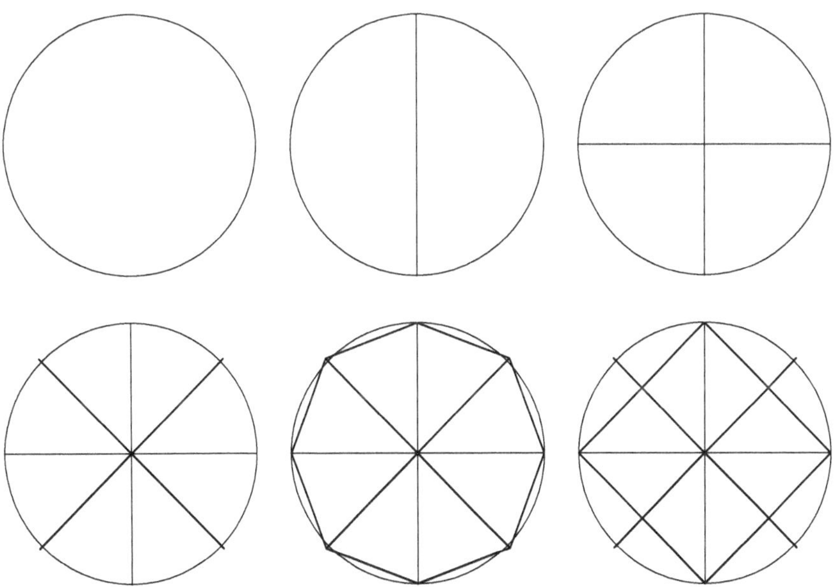

When I put the diagram in front of her, her eyes grew large in surprise but one corner of her mouth moved in an expression of incredulity, and more than just incredulity, it communicated that her Uncle Rick must have more than a few neurons firing uncontrollably.

I smiled at her and said, "It's true. This is what I saw."

It looked as if she still didn't believe me.

"It's on the video feed of six cameras."

Her face lit up.

"I also inadvertently caught a specimen."

At this, she sprang up, almost spilling her tea.

"Where is it?"

"It's in the library, under one of the cloches."

She ran away, leaving me alone to follow at my own, less speedy, pace.

Her trailing voice came back to me, "You might have lead with that!"

By the time I joined her upstairs in the library she was staring into the contents of the cloche, both hands raised to her head which she was shaking in disbelief, all the while saying, "Oh, my God! What is this? What is this? What in the world is this?" But I panicked when she asked, "Is it alive?"

I rushed over to the table and saw that the little creature was, indeed, sprawled on the saucer again. I had turned off the lamp when I went downstairs. In a moment of inspiration, I turned it back on so that it shone directly into the cloche. I also lifted the edge of the glass a bit and fanned it with my hand to get more oxygen in there.

Little by little the creature stirred, sat up, and began to glow.

"See? It's the light of the lamp that makes it glow. It doesn't glow by itself. Perhaps it cannot glow by itself. It needs a source of light."

"So it's glow-in-the-dark," Luna surmised. "Its skin contains phosphors that need to be energized. Although…"

There was that incredulity again. Luna was growing up to be an excellent scientist.

"Although…?" I asked.

"Although did you stop to think if it's the warmth from the lamp that reanimates her?"

"You might be right, yes, absolutely. Like a reptile that needs to bask in the sun. But the klieg lights last night were too far from the subjects to give them significant warmth." Then I remembered one of my conclusions of the night. "I have worked out the timing that the creatures need to become luminescent, and to maintain their glow independently of external light."

"You worked out the timing?" she asked me.

"More or less. Ten minutes of bright light will yield about a minute of luminescence."

"So… We have a case of phosphorescence here, then, rather than fluorescence."

"That is indeed my supposition."

I could see that Luna was beginning to observe the little creature itself rather than the light it emitted, and that the same things that had astounded me were now astounding her.

"This… this… this creature is like nothing else I've ever seen!"

"I know! I know! This is so incredible!"

She brought her hand to the side of the cloche. The little creature followed the movement with its stare and became alarmed when Luna's hand touched the glass.

"Obviously, it uses mimicry. Looks just like a painted bunting. It has no beak, though. It has lips, sorta… fish lips, hardly any nose, just a little bump with two nostrils. Its eyes, however, its eyes… They're so beautiful. Big and round, and blue. They're also bioluminescent.

"Look at the hands," I told her.

Luna gasped. "No, no, no… This isn't possible! How could this tiny creature have opposable thumbs? Uncle Rick! What's going on here? I'm having trouble believing in the existence of this creature, and yet… and yet, the evidence is right in front of me!"

"So now we know how the discoverers of the platypus felt, or the bioluminescent creatures of the deep."

"Yes, but could those animals dance?" she asked me.

"Want to see it?"

"Yes, of course."

In a minute I provided on the computer what she had asked for, replicated on six mini-screens. There were three pairs of eyes trained on the computer. The little creature seemed to be watching as well.

"That is absolutely fascinating," she said. "You can't really see the individual creatures, only the light they discharge. There is definitely a pattern there, to their movements. What's that sound, crickets?"

"You tell me," I coaxed.

She cocked her head in order to hear better.

"Holy moly!" she exclaimed. "It's them, isn't it? They're the ones generating the sounds, aren't they? It's in time to the movements, but it doesn't sound at all like music."

Luna increased the volume. The vocalizations of the dancing twinkles, if indeed they were produced by little vocal cords, filled the library: a fusing of clicks and pings together with what sounded like elongated sighs and moans. These last had an oscillating pitch. In the context of anthropological research, it could be called music. The fact that these were animals, perhaps we dared not call it music. The danger lurks for a scientist to anthropomorphize her subjects. And yet birds do create musical vocalizations. Dolphins and whales learn to sing, mimic each other's songs. Well, I didn't have time to delve into musical animals.

The little creature inside the cloche apparently could hear the calls well enough to react to them, for it had started to fly inside its glass enclosure. Of course it couldn't go anywhere. It just hovered within the bell jar, but as the "music" continued, it began to strike itself against the glass. Wham, and wham, it collided with the glass so that we feared for its safety.

"Turn off the volume," I cried out.

Luna hit the mute button immediately and the creature fell to the ground, breathing hard and resuming the position of pining despondency I had first identified.

"It looks sad," observed Luna. "How can that be?"

"How can that be, indeed, Luna," I answered with a big sigh. "I think that what we have here is an intelligence. This is no bug; this is no bird nor mammal. This is a sentient creature that reacts similarly to humans in certain situations. It is acting in such a manner now that I'm beginning to feel very guilty for having apprehended it. We're going to have to release it."

Luna was looking at the little thing with sympathy and concern.

"Yes," she said. "I agree. I agree with your assessment that this creature has feelings. Yet, this is why I think we should hold on to it a little while longer. I'd like… I'd like to… make an attempt to communicate with it. If it is indeed an intelligence, if they do indeed make music and dance to it, perhaps it would be able to… to… to communicate with us. Don't you think, Uncle Rick? Don't you think we should make an attempt?"

"I don't know. You may be right. But in the meantime, we need to change her container. This one doesn't let air in. I assume she needs oxygen like the rest of us."

"Ah, so it's a 'she' now, no longer an 'it'! Okay, I accept. I have the whole afternoon and evening free. Let's set her up in more comfortable surroundings and let's make the attempt to talk to her."

I smiled at Luna and nodded in complete agreement. I wanted to see if the little thing had the intelligence, and the linguistic capacity, to share its thoughts with another species. We had come this far with the little creature, raising her level up the ladder of Animalia, from Insecta to Ave, to Amphibia, to Reptilia and Mammalia, up to a higher sphere where feelings, sentiments, and thoughts play a part. Perhaps the mysterious little creature could feel. But could she communicate?

Friday, April 10, approximately 4 pm

An hour later, we had exchanged the cloche for a cage I had once used for Japanese quail chicks. Those day-old chicks were so small that an ordinary finch cage would have been of little use. Japanese quail babies were like walking balls of fluffy feather the size of a nickel, so we were confident that our little creature would not be able to get out. Before we put her in, we dressed up the cage with greenery, a small branch from an oak, some gardenia flowers, some ornamental kale, a bowl of water, a bowl of honey, and some romaine lettuce in case she was a vegetarian, some cat kibble in case she preferred that. We had no idea what she used for sustenance. But now, at least, she would be able to breathe and drink.

We also had changed rooms. We were now downstairs at the breakfast room table where we had more space and natural light. At our disposal were pads of drawing paper, writing implements, a smartphone to use as a recording device, an iPad for access to the Web, and a couple of magnifying glasses. We did not forget the desk lamp which we shone in her direction. A camera was tracking everything that went on inside the cage. We were ready.

The first thing we did was draw simple sketches of natural stuff, like a tree, a flower, an elephant ear leaf. We had no idea if she would recognize rudimentary pictures or even if she would react to them. She broke out in excited chatter when she saw those. When we drew animals, butterflies and snails, she responded with busy vociferations and body vibrations. But when the animals were owls, mice or foxes, she became silent and assumed a posture of fright, if not outright paralysis or cowering. We removed those images from her sight right away. She preferred flowers and trees, and a picture of rain falling from a cloud seemed to send her into raptures.

Over the next couple of hours we elicited numerous types of sounds from her. We call them sounds because we could not call them vocalizations or enunciations. It was not known to us if she used a larynx to emit her trills, whirrs and warbles. Insects buzz and frogs inflate their air sacs to croak; birds use their syrinx to chirp and twitter in a myriad of ways; but none of them has a larynx. We didn't know how this creature was producing her sounds. For all we knew she could be rubbing her legs together like a couple of miniature saws, similar to crickets that create sound by stridulating parts of their wings together. But chirping was only a minor part of the Little Thing's repertoire. She produced so many types of sounds in such quick succession that it was difficult to identify each single one. This was funny, for that is just the criticism that learners of a foreign language direct at native speakers of the target language. They say their speech all runs together and they can't tell when one word ends and the next one begins. So it was for us with the communication of the Little Thing. We were glad to be taping her twittering and rasping for slow playback at some future date.

The sounds made by the Little Thing had to be communicative in nature; they were too numerous, and too varied, not to be intentional and purposeful. She was loquacious. The Little Squirt sounded like an animated gossip with lots to tell, at times sounding exasperated, especially when she discoursed while exhaling but also while inhaling. Too bad Luna and I couldn't understand a thing. Her speech was far from human. It sounded more like a mix of the screeching of a cicada and a warbling of a bird. Sometimes it sounded like someone strumming the teeth of a comb. Every once in a while there was a hiss that sounded serpentlike, only of much shorter duration.

We started to classify the sounds she made. There were those produced by friction, like clicks and clacks, creaks, snaps, sneezes, and chittering. In this, we had the examples of the chirps of crickets and the squeaks of frogs, or even the creaking of boughs of a tree rubbed together by the wind. But the voiced sounds, where it seemed that vocal cords inside a tiny syrinx were vibrating, sounded otherworldly, like peeps of a chick, hoots of an owl, moans, titters, sighs, guttural trills or tremulous wheezes. Sometimes, along with the short hisses, she emitted a sound like fizz escaping slowly from a carbonated drink. There was another one, lasting for a couple of seconds, that sounded like the shivering of dry leaves on a branch. In these instances, too, there was a wide variety in pitch. To a linguïst it did sound like language, a very exotic one that wove sibilant fricatives with tonal wails interrupted by twittering chirrups and ending with low humming and high-pitched thrumming.

It was comical in its effect, and both Luna and I couldn't help bursting out in laughter. This reaction was apparently not to the Little Thing's liking. She erupted in an even more energetic bout of gibbering that left us spellbound.

At this rate, we were never going to understand what she was saying, or rather, uttering. We assumed she was upset, we assumed it was because we had removed her from her natural environment and were confining her. We would be upset, too, but the scientists in us could not now allow us to liberate her, at least not until we had some idea as to what we had found in our garden. Not least in our minds was the wish to name a new species and become famous among the taxonomic biologist crowd. But the most important thing was to understand a finding new to us, out of scientific curiosity and inquisitive discovery. We meant no harm. We would release her soon. Of that we were convinced.

We were also convinced that we would be thought of as hoaxers if we ever told anybody of our discovery without including convincing proof. But even if all the chittering that the Little Pipsqueak was emitting was on tape, as well as all her bioluminescent shimmering, videos were known to be easy to tamper with, especially these days with the ease of computer-generated imagery; our scientific legacy would be suspect. Our Little Specimen vociferated and ranted with energy, but after a while she relented and quieted down. Her insistent claims and spirited arguments, however eloquent and persuasive they may have been to her and her kind, were falling on non-appreciative ears.

Then the Little Thing did something that left Luna and me floored with astonishment. With her upper pair of legs, which I suppose could also be called arms, she began a series of movements. Luna grabbed a magnifying glass as I did too, and we instantly trained them on this Little Bug that was virtually squirming with repeated and purposeful motions that seemed to have the design of communication that gestures do. This Little Creature was sending us signals. Luna's jaw had dropped, and I realized mine had as well. What was this Little Being trying to communicate to us? It was now obvious to us that she had something to impart to us, information or knowledge, an idea or an emotion, some sort of intelligence to be transmitted from her to us, with the use of hand or arm signals. Her repetitive gestures required her right upper arm and both middle arms. While these three arms remained stationary in front of her, her three hands side by side in a row, palms up and their fingers held together, her left upper arm described repetitive, circular motions over them, perhaps as of someone writing, or drawing. Then with both pairs of upper and middle arms outstretched to her sides, she circumscribed arcs that first pointed towards us, then ended up at her thorax. It looked like she was inviting us to give her something. Then she dropped the three arms in front of her while the fourth described the motions of writing.

"Is it possible?" I asked.

"She wants us to give her writing tools."

"How can we give her writing tools? A pencil or a pen will crush her!"

"Well, we'll give her this." Luna had already grabbed a pencil and broken off the piece of lead at the end. She dropped it at the front of the cage, then she grabbed a piece of paper from a notepad, tore off a piece, and dropped that into the cage. The Little Thing ran to the materials, grabbed an edge of the paper and dragged it to the middle of the cage as if it were a heavy Oriental carpet. She returned to the piece of lead but could not lift it.

Luna quickly bit off some of the wood at the end of the pencil, managed to get a little bit more lead out, and crushed the piece under the side of the pencil. Smaller pieces broke off. Luna took one of the smaller pieces and dropped it into the cage. The Little Thing was able to lift it and run back to the piece of paper. She began to draw. Mostly it was scribbles that looked like repeated concave arcs, with a larger object in the middle that remained untouched by them.

"What is that?" I asked.

"I don't know. I can't tell," answered Luna.

The squiggles of repeating arcs went on and on, horizontally and vertically on the piece of paper, but the object in the middle remained white.

Luna unfurrowed her brow. "Those are waves," she said. "They are waves of water, flowing in all directions."

"So that thing in the middle, untouched by the waves, must be an island," I conjectured.

We were surprised by a tiny chittering coming from our Little Guest, or I suppose it must be said, our Little Prisoner. We took up our magnifying glasses and saw that her two middle arms were clapping. She was telling us that we were right.

"So she understands us?" asked Luna in amazement.

"That is what it looks like," I answered. "I can't believe it."

Turning my attention to the Little Being, I asked, "This is an island, then?" I asked her. "In the middle of the waves?"

She clapped even faster. Then she pointed to herself with four arms, walked to the middle of the island, and plopped herself down. She was sitting on the island.

Luna and I looked at each other. We were both bewildered. What could this possibly mean, and what was the importance of such a communication, seeing that it was the very first one that the Little Thing attempted?

We looked through our magnifying glasses again. When she knew we were again examining her, she clapped her four upper arms to her chest again, then brought them down on the depiction of the island.

"She has come to the island, or will come to the island," said Luna. "There are no tenses here. But the import of her message is that she comes to the island. Perhaps she already went to the island. Perhaps she is telling us that she comes from an island. Oh, dear," my niece looked at me with dismay. "Where, or what, is this island? Why is it of importance to her? And is this enigma meant for us to… to… decipher? Interpret? How are we supposed to react to this information?"

We noticed that the Little Bug had stopped clapping. She had dropped off the island and was now making swimming motions, with all six limbs, tracing a movement with her whole body towards the edge of the piece of paper. Where the ragged edge ended, she crawled the rest of the way, using all six appendages, to a back corner of the cage and sat down. She looked disconsolate.

We were also saddened by this failure to communicate. But the fact that there had been an attempt at all was a momentous occurrence in the annals of science. Thinking of science got me further depressed. Science only works when it is shared, communicated to others. Those others then attempt to replicate the data and find if it can be confirmed or disputed. But with only one Little Creature being examined, who would believe us? The fact that we had no credentials in any scientific discipline was also an obstacle. Luna was taking pre-med biology and organic chemistry in college, so she had access to her professors. I, on the other hand, had an influential friend, Dr. James Skutch of the local Audubon Society office in South Miami. He was a bona fide scientist, a good friend, and furthermore, he was discreet.

Friday, April 10, approximately 6 pm

*L*una and I stayed in the kitchen and helped ourselves to another cup of tea while we discussed what I would tell Jim once I called him. I happened to glance over at the media room and saw that the TV was turned on.

"That is so strange," I observed. "The TV keeps turning itself on," I told Luna. "It started about a week ago and this is the fourth or fifth time it happens."

"Maybe a neighbor has the same kind of TV and his remote is also affecting yours."

"I thought of that, but then there would certainly be other manifestations of the problem. You would think that as I was watching TV, the channel would change spontaneously, or go into menus and choose other programs, or fast forward, rewind or pause what I was watching. The only evidence that something is affecting this TV is that it comes on by itself. Why doesn't it ever turn off by itself?"

Luna considered the problem as I walked into the media room to retrieve the remote and turn the TV off. Whenever Luna was deep in thought she would bite her lower lip. "Still," she mused, "at what distance could a neighbor's remote be and still be able to control your TV? I've no idea of the range of infrared signals."

"Nor do I, but I know I can open the garage door from about half a block away."

"Well, there's a way to reconfigure your remote so it can't happen anymore."

She took the remote from my hand and went to her phone to look up the information. While she was employed with that task, I took a deep breath and used my phone to call Jim.

"Hi, Jim. It's Rick."

"Hey there, fella. Watchyou got?"

"Well, remember that conundrum I called you about on Wednesday?"

"The animal that burrowed in the leaf litter then jumped up and flew away?"

"Yes, that's the one. Well, I have more to tell you about it. I… It… Well, uhm… There's no more doubt about what it is. Or rather, there is still doubt, but… Oh, hell. I need to tell you this, Jim. I caught it."

"Ah, that's great! What is it, then? Is it a bird?"

"Well, no. It has no feathers."

"So it's a moth."

"It's not that, either, Jim."

"Well, then, more broadly, is it an insect?"

"Not unless there are insects out there without exoskeletons."

"No, my friend. All arthropods have rigid exoskeletons, or they couldn't exist."

"Well, what I caught does exist. I wasn't right about it being brown, but it does have blue and yellow, and its abdomen is a bright orange-red. And it seems to have purple wings."

"It seems to?"

"Well, it depends on the light, and the angle of the wings, but, yes, they are mostly purple. A beautiful, iridescent purple."

"So, is it a butterfly? A Morpho, maybe. But I can't see a butterfly burrowing in the leaf litter."

"Well, no. We've already established that this creature has an endoskeleton."

"So, it's a bat? A bat? It had dropped into the leaf litter? It certainly couldn't have been burrowing in it. Maybe it was just trying to get out. But what kind of bat has iridescent purple wings?"

"And what kind of bat is blue and yellow and red! It's not a bat. It's not a bat. It's something else. And you're going to have to come over and see it because I have no idea what it is."

After a few seconds of silence, Jim said, "How's about now? I'll come over now."

"I'll have a cup of tea waiting for you."

After I hung up, Luna came to me and handed over the remote.

"It's done. Wasn't too hard. Just had to change the frequency."

"Thanks, my dear," I said. "Jim is on his way."

"Great!" answered Luna. "I know he'll throw light on the subject."

Just at that moment, the TV came back on, all by itself.

The Tropical Audubon Society house is located on Sunset Drive, also called Marjory Stoneman Douglas Drive, in South Miami, within walking distance of my house. Marjory Stoneman Douglas, the famous environmentalist and defender of the Everglades, had lived just a few blocks away. Fresh with a degree in ornithology, Jim Skutch came down from New England in the 1980s after having read her landmark book, *The Everglades: River of Grass*, fell in love with the swamp and with the Tropical Audubon Society and never left.

Had Jim driven, it would have taken him three minutes to come over. But since he, of all people, made a conscious effort to lower his carbon footprint, he usually walked everywhere, even though his car, of course, was completely electric. It still took him less than ten minutes to walk over, so pressed was he by curiosity to see the creature I had caught.

The Tropical Audubon Society calls itself South Florida's Voice of Conservation. Its mission is to conserve and restore South Florida ecosystems, focusing on birds, other wildlife, and their habitats. They are the leaders in serving the public through their efforts on conservation, and they educate people on how to preserve the natural habitat in their yards and how to be responsible users of public parks. Besides habitat sustainability in Biscayne Bay, Florida Bay and the Everglades, they also focus on water quality for South Florida residents. Jim has been with them for decades and he takes his job seriously. Nature has no better protector than James Skutch.

As promised, I handed Jim a cup of strong tea as soon as he walked in the door. He greeted Luna with warmth and enthusiasm. He's been watching her grow up her whole life and has been instrumental in guiding her education. After a couple of sips of his tea, Jim, always impatient, always purposeful, got to the matter at hand.

"Let's see it, then," he said.

Luna and I led him into the breakfast area and gestured toward the cage.

Luna announced, "And now, introducing…" She hesitated for maximum effect. "The Little Thing!"

Jim bent down and peered into the cage. Luna and I held our breath. I knew Jim wore contact lenses, so I was puzzled when he picked up one of the magnifying glasses and began to examine the cage up and down, left and right. I became worried when he snapped, "Well, what am I supposed to be looking at, exactly?"

Simultaneously, Luna and I stooped over the cage. Luna had her magnifying glass, I had to grab mine from Jim's hand. We looked everywhere, even behind the oak leaves, the gardenias and the kale, searching low behind the bowls of water, honey and cat kibble. We followed the oak branchlet all the way up to its tip, but there was no Little Creature.

"Oh, no," I said. "She's escaped! How is it possible? The spaces between the wires are so narrow! Maybe she can squeeze even through those?"

"You're calling it a she, now?" asked Jim.

"You are not going to believe this, Jim. Yes, I'm calling her a she," I said as I opened the door to the cage and began gently picking up leaves and flowers and bowls to see where she could be hiding. She had vanished.

Jim took pity on us, we must have looked so crestfallen. "Well, tell me what it is that you saw. From the likes of your set-up here, you took video of, of… her. Time for playback."

We scrambled with the iPad to get into the home indoor cam security system, chose the right camera, and selected the point where we began our interview of the Little Thing.

Luna and I breathed a sigh of relief. It was all there. Our examination, our questions, the Little Thing's reactions to our questions, the piece of paper and the lead, her drawing, her mime. Instead of watching the camera view, Luna and I watched Jim's face. It had taken on a pallor that was troubling. His jaw had dropped five seconds into the video and would not go back up. We fast forwarded to the different scenes because we couldn't wait for his reaction to each of the stages. He had to sit down during the scene where the Little Sprite is miming the swimming motions.

"Those are waves. They are waves of water, flowing in all directions"; "So that thing in the middle, untouched by the waves, must be an island," we heard ourselves saying on the tape.

The video ended. Jim was speechless. Luna and I were excited to have shared our discovery.

"So, you see, Jim," I ventured. "I think I've discovered something important."

Jim looked at us as if this were the understatement of the year. He looked back at the cage, now with its door open. He lifted a hand and swung the door back and forth.

"I'll say you've discovered something important." He brought both hands up to his temples and released an "Aaah" of incredulity, of exasperation, of the frustration that a scientist feels when the subject of his study is not within his reach.

"Rick…, Luna…," he said slowly and calmly. "I want to know what you know. I want you to tell me the whole story, beginning to end. I want to start by seeing where you captured the…, the…, what are you calling it?—the Little Thing?—this life form I just saw communicating, rather, attempting to communicate, with humans. With us."

"Have the rest of your tea, Jim. I'll tell you the whole story. I won't be leaving anything out."

It took a while to apprise Jim of the whole narrative, along with an excursion into the front yard where the cameras were still set up and the elephant ear leaf still gleamed in the lengthening shadows. I explained the night lights and the dancing. I described the bioluminescence. I showed him the leaf litter under the elephant ear. I showed him the oak tree cavity where I had captured the Little Thing. Throughout my report, Jim looked like he was going to be sick. He kept nodding his head, perhaps in agreement or comprehension, or maybe just in acknowledgment, I don't know.

"Yeah, okay," he said when I was done. "Okay, then."

Jim left a bit absent-mindedly. He neglected to say good-bye to us. He just walked away from us, opened the gate, and continued on his way to the Audubon House.

"He's upset," I told Luna.

"I know. I would be, too. It's hard for a scientist to realize that, all of a sudden, there is a living organism, a life form, thrust into his awareness, that does not match anything else he's ever known. But now we'll never know, will we? It's gone. Such a tiny thing can hide anywhere. For all we know, when we opened the front door, it could have escaped outside."

"We do have the video."

"Will that be enough?"

I shrugged. "Well, at least, it's enough for us. What I want to do now is study it. Let's see if we can figure out how the Little Thing's communication works. This is a job for us linguists."

We went back into the house. With all the excitement, we had forgotten to have lunch. We were famished. While Luna went into the fridge to scrounge around for something to eat, I went back to the breakfast table. The cage looked forlorn and—

My shout brought Luna to me with a knife and a jar of mayonnaise in her hands. "What is it, Uncle Rick? What is it?"

There, inside the cage, with its door still wide open, was the Little Thing, bent over the honey bowl, sipping daintily at the golden amber liquid.

FRIDAY, APRIL 10, APPROXIMATELY 7:30 PM

There she was. The Little Thing was calm and serene, bowing low to bring her mouth to the honey. We could hear faint lapping sounds.

"She has a tongue," murmured Luna.

"She has a sweet tooth," I replied.

The Little Thing took a pause and looked straight at the open door of the cage but ignored it. I didn't bother to close it. She didn't seem to want to escape. As Luna and I watched, the Little Unknown Creature leaned on the edge of the bowl of honey, her six legs tucked neatly beneath her and her wings fully closed against her back, although we detected a slight pulsating motion to them as she sipped. I wish I could see her mouth to know how she was imbibing the thick liquid. It certainly sounded as if she were lapping, rather than slurping or sucking. Did she have a long tubular tongue, like a butterfly?

Why hadn't she escaped? And where had she been all this time?

As if to answer our speechless bewilderment, after her sweet meal of honey, and after she wiped her lips with one of her middle legs, she walked to the oak branchlet and began to climb it. Mid-way she stopped between two small twigs. While we watched, she stretched her little body, lifted her wings above her head and bent their extremities perpendicularly to her body. Lastly, she opened just the ends of her wings and they became like two oak leaves at the end of the twig. In a matter of seconds, she had transformed herself into part of the branch. Luna and I understood that the Little Thing had never left the cage. She had disguised herself as a twig.

We laughed, we shrieked, we jumped up and down. The Little Thing retracted her wings and returned to her normal size and shape, crawling back down the branch. Once back down on the floor of the cage she seemed to twitter in a wheezing manner. Was that her laughter?

Portrait of Luna

Twelfth event:

It was time to call on another friend. I decided to call Joan-Agnes for help in interpreting the Little Thing's system of communication. Joan-Agnes and I had met studying linguistics at the University of Miami. She had continued her studies in anthropological linguistics whereas I went off into the field of French literature. She had written her dissertation on K'ekchí, one of the Mayan languages spoken in the highlands of Guatemala north of the capital, with its weird glottal stops. She also knew quite a bit about Xhosa, one of the click languages of South Africa. If anyone was prepared to shed some light on our Little Loquacious Creature, it would be Joan-Agnes. Luna and I hoped that her reaction would be less nonplussed than Jim's had been.

"What's the emergency?" she asked as soon as she walked in the front door. She looked at Luna, then at me. "Are you both okay?"

"Yes, we are," I answered. "We are certainly okay. Thanks for coming over right away. Have we spoiled your supper?"

"No, not at all. It's leftover night. It'll microwave in minutes. What's going on?"

After a pause to search for words I added, "We need your help in identifying, perhaps describing, conceivably recognizing expressions of what Luna and I suspect are a type of language."

"Oh? I'm intrigued already. Why do you seem reluctant to designate these expressions a language? Even grunts and groans can be called a language if there is communicative intent behind them. If there is a pattern to them, we could even call that grammar."

"You are speaking, of course, of human communication," I ventured.

"Well, yes, of course. But what are you telling me? Let's be clearer with our own communicative efforts here. You want me to identify animal language? What species?"

I didn't know how to respond. Luna took over the conversation.

"Maybe it would be better if you just heard these sounds, the better to understand. We don't know what species uttered them, but we do suspect that there is some… organization, maybe… a sort of design, linguistic design. The creature that made them might be an animal, I think, but we're definitely talking about an intelligent animal, one who understands images in a drawing, who can use gestures in the attempt to communicate, who experiences frustration when the communication is not successful."

"Have the two of you gone mad?" was Joan-Agnes's reply. "There is no animal on earth that can do all that with the exception of primates, but they have neither the brain wiring nor the vocal anatomy to use speech. Guttural sounds and hoots are not speech."

We couldn't answer her, knowing she was right.

She looked at us and laughed. "Oh, I see. You're pulling my leg. Aren't you? You're late by a week. April Fool's, right?"

"Follow us," I told her.

Once in the kitchen, Luna sat her down on a chair and I placed a cup of tea in front of her. Joan-Agnes saw the cage on the table and the rest, eyeing the magnifying glasses and the iPad and the lit lamp over the cage with a bit of trepidation.

"What do you have here, an experiment? I hope it's not bugs!"

She knew that Luna and I were always working on some sort of project. But we knew she was curious. Linguistics was her love, and our speaking in riddles about an intelligent animal using a plausible language surely got her imagination working.

"It's dolphins, right? You have recordings of dolphin calls? Whales? Whale songs? Please don't tell me it's parrots. Or mynahs! People think they can speak. Well, they can't. They parrot. There's the lyrebird. It can mimic car alarms and squeaky hinges on a gate. But there's no higher purpose to their calls that could even remotely be called a language."

"Is your tea hot enough?" I asked.

"Are you comfortable?" Luna asked.

"Yes, thank you. Very hot and quite comfortable."

I placed a notepad and a pencil in front of her.

"We want you to hear this, with an open mind, using your knowledge of linguistics, of morphology, phonetics, syntax, and semantics, to ascertain whether this is a type of speech…, of language…, of some sort of communication system."

"Oh, boy," said Joan-Agnes, sitting upright and stabilizing herself on the chair. "You guys are serious. Ok, then. I'm ready. Let her rip."

She grabbed the pencil and poised it over the notepad.

With the computer screen facing away from Joan-Agnes's view, Luna turned on the recording of the Little Thing's ranting and raving. At first, Joan-Agnes's face flashed expressions of pain or disgust, tinged with incredulity interspersed with moments of confusion. Several times she glanced at each of us in turn with looks of suspicion. She still wasn't sure if we weren't pulling her leg. But as the tape continued, Joan-Agnes's face recorded interest, then inquisitiveness, then earnestness. Soon, her pencil was dancing over the notepad as she wrote down her observations, her impressions, her conjectures. Luna and I smiled at each other with increasing excitement as Joan-Agnes quickly turned a page to continue writing, then turned another page, and then another. After the session ended, Joan-Agnes had filled six pages with her scribblings. Of course, she had also heard the words of our own conversation, which meant that she had to have realized that there was some sort of interaction between the creature and us.

Joan-Agnes looked at the camera trained on the cage. "You have the video, don't you?" she asked us.

We could tell that she was going to rip the place apart if she didn't see the video right away. Luna turned the screen around to face her and pressed replay. While the video played, Joan-Agnes stared wide-eyed at the creature who was emitting the sounds of an unknown language. What surprised Luna and me was that when the creature looked despondent and drooping, apparently disappointed in the failure to communicate, fat tears spilled from Joan-Agnes's eyes and ran down her cheeks. After the video was over, all she could do was drink her tea.

When she seemed to be more collected, she said to us, "Why is the door on the cage open? Where's the… where's the… the…"

Luna finished her question. "The Little Thing?"

"She's in there," I replied. "She's definitely in there. Although… she may not want to show herself to you."

Joan-Agnes looked puzzled.

"We don't know if she will allow you to see her," said Luna. "Jim was here before, and the creature hid from him. We thought she had escaped, but she was inside the cage all along. She is a master of camouflage."

We all stared at the cage. The Little Thing crawled down from her perch on the oak branch, walked upright on her hind legs to the bowl of honey, and sat down on its edge, as calm as calm could be.

Thirteenth event:

FRIDAY, APRIL 10, APPROXIMATELY 9 PM

Joan-Agnes took pity on the Little Creature and stuck her hand in the cage, startling Luna and me.

"It's okay," she said. "She showed herself to me."

With forefinger outstretched, Joan-Agnes placed it in front of our Little Friend and the miniature Little Being hopped aboard. Joan-Agnes retrieved her hand and held it up to her face.

"Hi, there, Little Thing! How are you? What are you? You're a little fairy, aren't you?"

Luna and I were alarmed, I more than Luna.

"Joan-Agnes… Joan-Agnes… What are you doing?" I asked her.

Joan-Agnes looked at me with the joy of wonder in her eyes and a wide smile on her lips. "Well, she looks like a fairy. She looks as if she's just stepped out of a fairy book from the Nineteenth Century."

"There's no such thing as fairies," I berated her. "They're mythological creatures!"

"So, what? You disbelieve your eyes? They're your very own eyes! What are they telling you? You do a great disservice to science. You have the evidence in front of you. There's no leap of faith needed here. We can see her, hear her. I can feel her two little feet on my finger; she has weight, but not much! And… and this close to me, I can smell her. She smells like vanilla!"

She turned her attention back to the Little Thing and continued speaking to her. "You are a little fairy, aren't you?"

The Little Thing responded by deploying her iridescent blue wings, uttering a soft trilling sound, and fluttering upward a couple of inches from Joan-Agnes's finger.

"She is absolutely beautiful!" admired Joan-Agnes. "And see? If that isn't a communication of agreement I don't know what is."

Luna and I had to concur.

The Little Thing settled again on her finger.

"She showed herself to me," continued Joan-Agnes. "That means she trusts me. I don't believe she trusted Jim. Jim is tall and big and gruff, and his voice is assertive and, well, loud. We know Jim has a good heart, but how would this Little Creature know, huh? Yes, you're a tiny, tiny cute Little Fairy, aren't you? And you're very clever not to show yourself to people you don't trust. We always hide from big lumbering brutes, don't we? We're afraid of big noisy people."

The Little Fairy-thing warbled its approval again. Joan-Agnes pronounced a long French r, vibrating the fricative produced by the soft palate and the back of the tongue. Her Little Friend trilled its own syrinx, or whatever it was that she had in her throat.

"You're not going to show yourself to just anybody, are you? Only to people who love you and care for you and find you so very, very cute, you cutie, oh, my clever little cutie."

Joan-Agnes actually started to make kissing sounds, which the Little Thing mimicked right back with her plump little fish lips.

"Oh yes, oh yes, oh yes. You only show yourself to people you trust and who love you. You know to trust me, don't you, you Little Cutie. You can trust Auntie Joan-Agnes. You can call me Auntie Joan if you like. But tell us, what is your name? You have a name, don't you? I'm sure you do."

The Little Thing opened its lips and, interspersed with strange clicks and airy sibilants, she clearly said, "Celesta."

I thought I was going to faint. Luna started to clap. Joan-Agnes brought the Little Thing, who now had a name, closer to her face as if it were a little budgerigar and kissed her on top of her little head.

Fourteenth event:

FRIDAY, APRIL 10, APPROXIMATELY 10 PM

Joan-Agnes never did go home to supper. She was too enthralled, as were we, by this successful interchange of information. No one was hungry, save for little Celesta. Every now and then she would fly into her cage to sip more honey. When I brought the bowl of kitty kibble closer to her, she turned up her nose at it, or rather her nostrils, since she didn't have a projecting proboscis like the rest of us. I removed the kibble, as well as the romaine. She did want to keep the gardenia. She would go to it periodically and take in huge drafts of inhalation.

Luna and I looked at each other.

"She has an olfactory system," said Luna.

"She has lungs," I said.

"Plus, she has, what seems to me, both a larynx and a syrinx," added Joan-Agnes.

"That would explain a lot."

We looked down at Joan-Agnes's notes.

"So, tell us, dear linguist," I exhorted. "What hast thou heard, from all this twittering and rasping, chirping and trilling, that would convince us that what Celesta is uttering might rightfully be called language."

Joan-Agnes took on her professorial attitude in her answer.

"It is language, absolutely a language, but very different from ours. Still, I might point out, most people are surprised when they learn that human languages differ so much one from the other, not just in the sounds we use to produce them, but in the manner in which we manipulate the sounds that make up the language. Some human languages are to linguists as mysterious and fascinating as luminous fish from the bottom of the sea are to ichthyologists, or blind, albino salamanders living in remote caves are to speleologists."

She took a momentary pause to look at her notes.

"All the sounds that we produce, with few exceptions, I find in Celesta's speech. The only ones missing are the nasal consonants and vowels. No m's or n's, no *eñes* (here she switched to Spanish to produce the ñ sound), and no ã, ɛ̃, ɔ̃, or œ̃ (here she switched to French to pronounce its four nasal vowels). Everything else that humans emit in language is there, plus she adds a whole lot more. Oh, boy, a whole lot more, an absolute plethora more. You're right about the trilling and the chirping. It sounds as if this language has appropriated for itself the vocalizations of birds. The two systems, bird language and human language, seem to lie side by side, with no separation, forming a seamless, continuous coordination. Other elements of language are intact. There is stress, or emphasis, on certain syllables, and there seems to be tone and inflection, repetitive intonation patterns, voiced consonants, fricatives, many, many glottalized vowels, etc., etc.

"However, I find two very interesting things about Celesta's communication, and these are very, very different from our own way of vocalizing. First, I don't encounter any diphthongs anywhere in her speech. There are never two vowels pronounced one directly after the other, so no 'ows' or 'eyes' or 'wahs'; vowels are always separated by the consonants that we use in English, save for the nasal ones, or by full glottal stops, as in the German *der Apfel* or in *k'ekchí*, from the Guatemalan indigenous language K'ekchí, where the airway closes up. Furthermore, her enunciations seem always to end with a vowel. Ending with a vowel is just like Italians speaking in English; they add a slight puff of a vowel to all our words ending in a consonant, redə, blackə, dogə. Look at Celesta's name: no diphthongs, ends with a vowel. On the other hand, I find many instances where three, four, even five consonants pile up in a row. So, we can definitely make the observation that this is a language with few vowels, only seven, in the mix. They are /a/, /e/, /i/, /o/, /u/, /ə/, and /y/. (I am using the International Phonetic Symbols here.)"

Luna and I recognized this last vowel from French or German, which sounds like a combination of /u/ and /i/.

"So," continued Joan-Agnes, "with so many consonants, especially fricatives, it is difficult to compare this language with human languages. But if you want some human examples that approximate this, look to Russian or Polish. French would be the opposite. French does not allow for the pronunciation of three consonants in a row, let alone four or five."

Joan-Agnes paused to allow us to soak the information in.

"Wow!" we both said in admiration.

"*Tsatsa!*" exclaimed Celesta, who was now sitting on top of her cage.

"See?" exclaimed Joan-Agnes. "She cannot begin a word with a 'w' because for all intents and purposes that sound is a vowel. Neither can she produce three vowels in a row! So, your 'wow' becomes her *tsatsa*. Isn't that right, clever little Celesta? 'Wow' is *tsatsa!*"

"*Tsatsa!*" repeated Celesta. We laughed in amazement. Still, I couldn't quite understand if Celesta's exuberantly pronounced *tsatsa* was a translation of the interjection 'wow' into her own language or if it was her attempt to pronounce our 'wow.' The two words seemed so far apart, like long-lost cognates that had diverged to an unintelligible degree. Yet I understood Joan-Agnes's premise, that certain foreign sounds are difficult, or even impossible, to pronounce. Asians have trouble differentiating between 'r' and 'l'; Spanish speakers have trouble discerning the difference between the English words 'pen' and 'pin,' let alone trying to produce them; and I have never been able to mimic, to my satisfaction, anyway, the Russian vowel 'ы' or the Arabic pharyngeal consonant 'h,' both of which seem to come from deep within the throat.

"What's your second observation?" asked Luna.

"Well, did you notice that when Celesta 'speaks,' and I am willing to call it that, she does so while exhaling, just like we do, but she also continues to speak, with no apparent change in quality to her voice, while inhaling, which we can force ourselves to do, but it sounds very weird, very unnatural. I find Celesta's mode of communication to be quite economical. There are no pauses during inhalation."

"Wow!" admired Luna. "You don't have to wait to catch your breath! You can speak twice as fast, get twice the amount of information in."

She proceeded to demonstrate to us how a human would do it. While exhaling she said, "I would love to be able to speak faster." Then while inhaling she said, "People would really have to pay attention to me." Then she exhaled again: "And I would always have the last word!"

We all laughed, including Celesta. That strange tremulous wheezing sound she emitted was, apparently, her laughter.

"She understands humor," I observed.

Luna added, "She understands bonding."

Fifteenth event:

FRIDAY, APRIL 10, MIDNIGHT

It was very late when Joan-Agnes finally went home. She had to wrench herself away from Celesta who preferred to perch on Joan-Agnes's shoulder as we discussed our next moves. We wondered what we next should do with Celesta. Should we keep her for a while longer? Should we release her? Should we alert the zoology professors at the University of Miami? Should we write our own paper to introduce Celesta as a new species, perhaps a new genus, perhaps a new taxonomic family?

I wanted to keep Celesta while we considered our options. She didn't seem to be uncomfortable now in our presence. She looked quite relaxed on Joan-Agnes's shoulder. Every ten or fifteen minutes Celesta would fly to her honey saucer and at times fly to the top of her cage to absorb light from the lamp. Whenever she did so, she would glow with a luminous rosiness. Were we to release her, I told them, we would worry about her safety. I mean, if a bumbling human had been able to catch her, wouldn't a fox be a greater threat, or a hawk, or even a cat? At night there were owls and raccoons. Luna wondered if there were others of her kind outside with whom she could find safety. I had told Joan-Agnes and Luna about my experience when I first caught the Little Thing earlier that day. Out of the foliage, from the overhead canopy, from all over the garden rose a storm of clamoring that sounded like bickering and scolding. I can always tell when there's a fox, a hawk or a snake in the yard because all the songbirds start to twitter up a maelstrom. What I had heard when I captured Celesta from the hollow of the tree had been of an exponentially higher order. It was disconcerting and even threatening. I immediately surmised it was her species complaining about my rude appropriation of their little companion.

I've always felt that when in doubt, one should go to the source. We asked Celesta herself many questions, about her kind, their numbers, where they lived, how they lived, how long they had been there, etc. Although she seemed to understand us with no problem, when she would respond to our questions, there was absolutely no way for us to interpret even the slightest little bit. We taped a long segment of our "conversation" with Celesta, with the intention that Joan-Agnes would take it home and study it. I had great confidence that if anybody could make some headway in the fairy's language it would be she.

Yes, I finally capitulated and started calling the Little Thing a fairy. I hoped that by doing so it wouldn't open the floodgates to all sorts of critters appearing in the garden, like trolls, nymphs and leprechauns. I don't mention hobbits because I know them to truly be a fabricated, novelistic, creation. But I felt that there was a danger here. When you accept one impossibility, don't you have to open your mind to others?

Shortly after Joan-Agnes left, Luna went to her bedroom upstairs. Little Celesta had fallen asleep inside her cage, so Luna took the cage, along with the lamp, with her to make sure the cats would not pose a danger. But she wasn't even out of the kitchen before I let out a yelp of surprise. She came running back.

I had just checked to see if both kitchen doors were locked and when I glanced at the pool area, I saw the pool lights were blazing on, including the rotating disc that makes them change color, and in addition, the pool fountains were all splashing away.

"Luna, by chance, did you turn the pool lights on?"

"I haven't been anywhere near one of the panels or remotes."

"Well, there's something weird going on. First the TV, then the lights in the house, now this. I'll have to call the tech guy. We have gremlins here."

With that word, gremlins, we both looked at Celesta curled up into a sleeping little ball inside the gardenia blossom. She looked like she belonged there.

SATURDAY, APRIL 11, MORNING

Three cats reside in the house. Lucy, the oldest, came with me the very day I moved in sixteen years ago. The day the moving truck came to pick up my things, her mother gave birth in the carport of the farmhouse where I had been living across the county. It all happened in a basket amidst the other stuff going to my new home. In an emergency, I had to take both mother and her four newborn kittens to the vet. For some reason, Aurelia, an itinerant Siamese mix, hadn't cut their umbilical cords and they became hopelessly entangled. Sadly, only one of them survived, so I called her Lucky, but the vet's assistant left out the k when she typed her name down and she became Lucy.

Lucy is the *grande dame* of the house. She moves regally, eats elegantly, and when she uses her litter box, she does not deign to cover her traces. She allows either Gracie or Milly to do that for her. She also is not very vocal. The only meow she emits sounds like a grumpy growl, which she uses when one of the other cats makes the faux pas of wanting to play with her, or when she benevolently acquiesces to allow me the paramount honor of petting her. But her deep soulful eyes that shine a brilliant blue gaze into my own eyes so laser-like that she looks through me and beyond me, as if she were looking at what I've done in the past or going to do in the future. If ever there was a cat who would be a benevolent familiar to a sorcerer, it would be Lucy.

Gracie came next, six years ago. Found in the middle of a feeding dish belonging to the outside cats, of which there are three, she was tiny, skinny, and voracious. She grew into an energetic, mischievous, gray tuxedo who loves to bother Lucy, but only receives growls in return. Then a tabby, Millie, short for Milagros, for she also was a miracle, was found on my farm in South Dade, age unknown but still youngish, almost dead trying to rear four kittens. She was very tame and I adopted her because I admired her courage and tenacity. Her cute kittens were readily adopted by neighbors.

My outside cats consist of Matt and Aaron, twin black feral cats born in the backyard, whose mother, Victoria, disappeared shortly after they became independent. There is also Lady Grey, a big gray tuxedo, and probably Gracie's mother, but so wild she would not allow herself to be put in a carrying case to be taken to the vet's. She does allow me to pet her on her back as I'm feeding her, but at no other time.

With the arrival of Celesta, I saw danger lurking in the jaws and claws of my little kitties. In my thoughts, I saw them everywhere lurking and stalking and attacking, then snacking and licking their chops. They were all super-well fed, especially Milly who is definitely overweight. But I know cats. It's not that they would be hungry for a dainty little morsel of a fairy, but they're adventurous, they're intrepid, and they're curious. Especially little Gracie. If Celesta was going to remain inside the house, we needed to do something about the cats. But I abhorred the idea of keeping the cats confined to a room, or even to a floor.

It turned out that there was no need to worry. The next morning Luna had gone into the bathroom to take a shower and inadvertently, or rather, in my opinion, insouciantly leaving her bedroom door open. When she came out of the bathroom, she froze in fear. Gracie had hopped onto the nightstand and was sitting in front of Celesta's cage. Luna coolly took her cell phone and shot a video, which she showed me a few minutes later in the kitchen.

Gracie was nudging at something, turning her head this way and that. That something turned out to be Celesta. Gracie was trying to bunt her with her head, but next to Celesta, Gracie's head was huge. Celesta had to use her wings to maintain her balance. Why Gracie wasn't fascinated with the blue whirring of the wings cannot even be surmised. But the two were acting like old friends, Gracie playing with what looked like a colorful moth, and Celesta hanging on to Gracie's whiskers for dear life, but seemingly enjoying the ride.

Gracie & Celesta

Seventeenth event:

Saturday, April 11, later that morning

Over coffee and honey, Luna and I decided we had to bring Jim Skutch back. We needed his expertise in examining Celesta physically as Joan-Agnes had observed her linguistically. But would Celesta allow him to see her, let alone grant him permission to inspect her?

Celesta was with us downstairs at the breakfast room table without her cage. We placed her honey dish between us and she kept buzzing between our shoulders and the dish, with a few side visits to soak up some light from the lamp. I had had the idea of rummaging through the garage to look for one of the heating lamps I used whenever I had chicks to raise, and Celesta loved it. She gave off an even stronger glow whenever she went under it.

I explained to little Celesta that I wanted to have my friend Jim back to see her. He was not a threat, I told her. On the contrary, he was a true friend of the environment. He loved nature and all the creatures in it and was instrumental in protecting all that belonged to the natural world. I showed Celesta the Tropical Audubon Society's website that proved how committed they were to help protect the environment. Celesta seemed to watch the iPad screen with interest. When I asked her if I could bring Jim back, she seemed to purr her affirmative reply.

Jim lost no time in returning. On the phone he kept running over his own syllables in the attempt to communicate what he had discovered by watching the video of Celesta when she had first been inside the cage. He kept saying that this discovery of a new species of animal was "spectacu— extraordi—unheard of— never in a million— I can't fathom— this is absolu— marve— incredible!"

Jim ran over from the Audubon House. Joan-Agnes drove up at the same time. She hadn't even called to say she was coming. In her arms was a stack of heavy books, all on linguistics by what I could read on the spines.

Jim and Joan-Agnes had met years ago through me. They were both die-hard conservationists and members of Friends of the Earth International, the Audubon Society, and the American Society for the Prevention of Cruelty to Animals, as was I. We were also sponsors of the Florida Keys Wild Bird Sanctuary. They had established their own friendship, traveling together to Costa Rica, South Africa, Iceland, New Guinea and other far-flung and exotic places to pursue their pleasure of birding and other wildlife observation. The only time I ever joined them was on a birding trip to the Canadian Rockies; I don't do too well far from hot showers and restaurants. I think this stems from a visit I once took to the Mayan ruins of Tikal where the accommodations were simple, clean and rudimentarily adequate, but it was impossible to keep the jungle out of the rooms. An arachnologist would have spent the day studying only the species of spiders I spotted in the shower stall.

It was Saturday so Luna had no classes at the university. Besides, what we were doing here with a newly-found species was more groundbreaking than any discoveries her professors had ever made. All four of us converged around the breakfast table to contemplate our rare finding. Joan-Agnes and Jim were entranced. They could only stare as Celesta whirred down from the ceiling where she had been perching on the chandelier. She landed next to her honey dish, looking shy and a bit nervous.

"Celesta," I said. "You already know Joan-Agnes. This is Jim from yesterday, the one you didn't allow to see you. He is a friend of nature and he absolutely loves birds. His grandfather, Alexander Skutch, was a famous ornithologist who wrote best-selling books about his experiences with tropical birds in Guatemala, Honduras, Costa Rica and Panama. Like I said before, you can trust him. He poses no danger. He just wants to understand you, just as we all do. Jim is an expert on all sorts of animals. His knowledge is positively encyclopedic."

She chittered at that, holding up her forearms, palms up, and wagging her right middle arm.

Joan-Agnes said, "I don't think she understood that last word, 'encyclopedic.' Let me explain: We people write down all the knowledge we have in books we call encyclopedias. Similar to these." She pointed to her books. "So when we say somebody's knowledge is encyclopedic, it means that the person knows many, many things about a certain subject. Jim has studied animals, especially birds, all his life."

Celesta clicked and spluttered her approval. She waved her upper arms up and down as if she were flying, saying [fl'gki/ʃky], whose closest approximation into English is *flgishku*. Joan-Agnes wrote the pronunciation down on a notebook as she observed, "Don't you find it funny that she didn't use her own wings as a gesture?"

Luna made a comment. "I don't think we should use the word 'animal' in our conversations with Celesta. That word connotes an otherness, a separation from humans that smacks of judgment and disparagement. It's like we've always wanted to make sure that everybody knows that we are humans and everybody else is an animal. Well, is that right? Is that the way it's supposed to be? Is that really the message we want to convey? We should instead say that Jim is an expert on our fellow creatures. If you wish to remain scientifically neutral, we can say that Jim is an expert on other species, of which humans are but one."

We all nodded our agreement. Little Celesta flew to Luna's shoulder and warbled softly.

I defended my use of the word 'animal' because I didn't mean it as a disparagement. "It's not an old word, this word 'animal': it stems from Middle English, from the Old French *anme*, meaning soul. So, originally, an animal is any thing, any being, that is able to animate itself, to move according to its volition, that has the breath of life and thus its own will to take action. I think it's a better term than the word it replaced, 'beast,' although I still think you're right, Luna. Most people continue to believe that humans are the only creatures who possess language and use tools and feel emotions, thus distinguishing us as people rather than animals. That mentality is truly disparaging to other creatures, and condescending, and downright ignorant. In the interest of uniting us with the other species, I would rather see the word 'animal' used to include us humans as well."

Everybody at the table agreed with me, including Celesta who whirred across the table to land on my shoulder.

Jim looked like he was about to keel over in his chair.

"Jim, are you okay?" asked Joan-Agnes.

"Yes, it's okay. It's just that… It's just that… this sort of thing doesn't happen. Now, if you told me that this little specimen of a species was from outer space, an extraterrestrial being, a…, a…, a… creature from another planet come to earth, I would find that easier to believe!"

Celesta wheezed in laughter.

"She finds that funny," said Luna. "As do I."

Joan-Agnes spoke to Jim, saying, "But it *is* happening, Jim. And we are the witnesses, or rather the observers of a wondrous occasion. We have been given this wonderful gift, a fellow being, *on earth*, who has been made visible to us. We must treat this gift with gratitude and respect. This has to remain with us. We cannot tell the world about any of this. Fairies are secretive beings. They don't appear to just anybody. No scientist has ever studied a fairy, let alone caught sight of one in the wild. If science had ever collected a fairy specimen from the wild, it would have been immediately pinned to a board or stuffed and mounted!"

Celesta gave out a little cry of anguish, so high-pitched it was nearly inaudible.

Joan-Agnes turned to Celesta and said, "Sorry, Celesta. But it's true. We cannot publish our findings. Not until we know more. We need more information."

Jim objected. "But science needs to know. We have a responsibi—"

Joan-Agnes cut him off. "Our only responsibility is to the safety and well-being of this little creature, who has given her trust to us. We have to honor that trust."

She brought her forefinger to my shoulder and Celesta hopped onto it. "Yes, we do, don't we, beautiful fairy. We can't just go blabbing about your existence all over the place! The world will beat a path to our door! Everyone will want to know, to see, to touch, to feel. But the really dangerous ones will be the ones who don't believe, who won't believe, who refuse to believe. Those people will cry out, 'Well, why are fairies not in the Bible, why weren't they on the Arc?' and all that rubbish. Those are the ones who will want to get rid of the evidence."

Joan-Agnes kissed Celesta on the head. Celesta kissed her right back, making sweet warbling noises that changed pitch like a beautiful, ethereal melody that was at once atonal and dulcet.

Luna asked the essential question.

"Well, then. If we were chosen to know about the existence of Celesta, we do need more information. We need to find out why. Why us?"

"I'm glad you asked that question," said Joan-Agnes, putting down her finger on top of her books. Celesta hopped onto the stack of thick heavy tomes. "I think I can learn Celesta's language. It shouldn't be that hard because she understands human language. She just needs to answer my questions. How do you say 'bird' in fairy language?"

Celesta responded, "*flgishku.*"

We all tried to pronounce it but apparently our efforts were so mangled that they resulted in a fit of wheezing laughter from Celesta.

"How do you say 'book' in fairy language?" continued Joan-Agnes.

Celesta answered with a twitter, a click, a pop, and the vowel /u/. It sounded like *rrkptu.*

Joan-Agnes imitated the series of sounds rather well.

Celesta wheezed and clapped with two sets of hands.

We all imitated it: a twitter, a click, a pop, and a /u/. *Rrkptu.*

"How do you say 'eyes'?" asked Joan-Agnes.

Celesta answered with the consonant /l/ followed by a vowel, /a/, then the glottalized /ts/ sound that humans use to chide each other, usually written as *tsk*, with a final vowel /a/. *La'tsa.* We all pronounced it.

Celesta wheezed her pleasure and whirred about the room. Then she stopped and hovered over the table. She used her right arms to beckon to us as she flew backwards away from the table and towards the middle of the kitchen. When we didn't react, she flew back to the table and landed on its surface. She sat down, then got up and walked to its edge. She again flew off and beckoned to us.

We all said in excited unison, "She wants us to follow her!"

We scrambled to our feet and walked after her as she led us to the front door of the house. She led us into the garden, close to the elephant ear. She began an excited chatter of fairyspeak, full of yattering and warbling and trilling. It was sweet music to our ears. After she was done, all was calm and silent.

SATURDAY, APRIL 11, LATER THAT MORNING

*I*t was a sunny, glorious spring day in South Florida, not too hot or humid. Celesta chittered a few more syllables and became quiet once more.

Slowly, a correspondence of similar calls rose up in the garden, in all directions, around us, above us, by our feet. At the same time, a hundred dry dead sticks, green leaves, stems, beetles, bumblebees, dragonflies, blossoms of many colors, and strands of Spanish moss came to life and took flight, fluttering and flickering in the sunshine. They all drifted towards us and before we knew it, a hundred hovering creatures were wafting around us in a dense swarm, closer and closer, creating a surreal effect of tiny helicopters glimmering and whirring in the air.

I will not sugarcoat the feeling I felt. If it wasn't fear outright, it certainly felt like apprehension. My adrenalin was flowing and I felt like swatting at the critters, but that might have made them mad as hornets. I saw the faces of my fellow humans and immediately recognized their own unease. Instinctively we began backing away from the swarm.

Celesta flew the closest to us, spluttering her little sounds to us, flitting from one to the other, trying hard to communicate, but our human instinct, too strong to ignore, was telling us that swarms of bees or wasps or unknown little things were something we had to avoid. We had gathered into a tight circle, clinging to each other as we slowly backed up to the front door.

All of a sudden we heard a clear voice, not Celesta's, somewhere amid the swarm. It rose up above the sound of fluttering. "Do not be afraid!" it said, in immediately recognizable English. "We will not harm you!"

But I don't think we were in any disposition at that moment to understand the meaning of the words uttered by the strange voice. All we could tell was that it was non-human. Jim lost his footing and fell on the paving stones of the driveway. Luna bent down to pick him up, but Jim enveloped her in his arms, as if to protect her, and brought her down next to him. Joan-Agnes was cutting off the circulation in my arm. I was feeling lightheaded. I thought this had to be an illusion, a figment of our overwrought imagination. Hundreds of Celesta-sized beings hovering and buzzing around us could not be real. And yet I saw little Celesta close to my face. I felt the weight of Joan-Agnes as she went down, too. We were having a fight-or-flight reaction in slow motion, but in our confusion of disbelief and distress, what had won out in our arsenal of instincts was a complete surrender to our peril. We embraced each other as we thought our final demise had come. Clutching each other, we all closed our eyes.

There was a high-pitched cry and all the buzzing ceased. It took us a few seconds to garner enough courage to open up our eyes again.

Nineteenth event:

The swarm was gone. No little being was anywhere to be seen. Had they all gone back to their hiding places in the trees and the shrubs? Did they all return to their positions as sticks and flowers and hanging moss?

We heard the new voice again. It was coming from the ground. We looked down and saw Celesta together with another figure of quite a distinct character. Taller than Celesta, stouter, too, was a green little thing who looked, to me, like nothing more than a katydid.

"I regret that we startled you," it was saying. "That was not our intention."

Luna was the first among us who could collect her wits fast enough to form a sentence.

"Who are you?" she asked.

"Please allow me to introduce myself. My name is Darragh. I am Celesta's father. I am so sorry that we startled you. It was not our intention. We meant you no harm."

"Where did everybody go?" asked Joan-Agnes, getting up from off her knees and dusting herself.

"They went back to their hiding places, as before," replied the funny little figure. If Celesta looked like some kind of bird-moth, her father looked like an arrangement of folded leaves, two big ones for his body and one for his head. This new little creature who spoke English had a voice almost as high-pitched as Celesta's, but gravelly and tremulous. It is hard to explain, but there was a secondary quality to his voice, like the sound of a saw cutting through wood and accompanying the primary voice.

The humans exchanged glances of relief and a few sighs. I don't know about the others, but I felt slightly ridiculous for having let trepidation get the best of me. Viewed rationally, it was silly to think that Celesta had maneuvered us outside only to be mauled by a horde of Little Things. I should have had more trust in Celesta.

What follows here is the conversation we had with Celesta and her father, Darragh. Well, it was only with Darragh since Celesta didn't speak English, although she seemed to be able to understand what was said.

I will forever be grateful to Joan-Agnes for having recorded the scene on her phone, for I would have forgotten the half of it. Joan-Agnes could not believe her ears that the little father creature was speaking in English, the Queen's English, very clear, very posh.

Twentieth event:

Rick: How is it that you speak English?

Darragh: We all learn the languages of the humans around us.

Joan-Agnes: How is it that you are able to understand human language?

Darragh: Simple. You make noises that impart meaning; we learn the meaning. In just this same way, we learn the meaning of the languages of others. You do not. You are indifferent to the languages of others. You cannot abide the possibility that others have language as well.

Joan-Agnes: You mean, like the languages of birds?

Darragh: Of birds, of mammals, of reptiles. There are whole conversations going on out there of which you are completely unaware. Not that it would matter if you did understand the languages of other creatures. You would ignore them anyway.

Joan-Agnes: But you do understand them?

Darragh: Of course! We learn the languages of our friends; we also learn the languages of our enemies.

Joan-Agnes: Is there such a thing as fairy languages, plural? Does a fairy from Florida understand a fairy from Iceland?

Darragh: Oh, yes, in the same way a Florida sparrow understands a European sparrow. Furthermore, cross-species communication is rampant. A Florida sparrow understands an Icelandic puffin, and so forth. Any squirrel will understand the alarm calls that the birds around them make at the sighting of a predator.

Joan-Agnes: Why do fairies even take the time to understand human speech?

Darragh: We have always needed to know what the enemy is saying. We cannot allow ourselves to be surprised by human intentions. But let me ask you a question: Are you not curious about why humans do not understand the language of other creatures? The fact that this question does not even occur to you proves the point that humans are selfish and arrogant. They do not accept the obvious fact that other creatures have language.

Jim: Do fairies look upon humans as the enemy?

Darragh: Of course, we do.

Jim: Why do fairies consider humans as their enemy?

Darragh: From the very beginning humans have been destructive. They would rather kill a creature that they do not understand rather than take the time to understand it. We fairies know that there are dangerous creatures in the world. But we have learned to keep our distance from them. Humans destroy many creatures because they fear them, without having a justification for their fear. Humans kill for sport, for the joy of killing. Also, they eat everything.

Joan-Agnes: Do you have written language?

Darragh: Yes, we do, but we only transmit our messages ephemerally. We write on flower petals with tree sap, or we arrange little sticks on the ground, nothing that lasts. We do not want to leave evidence of our existence for humans to find. Also, what we write is mostly about where to find the juiciest blossoms, or warn about nearby dangers. We transmit our wisdom orally from the elders to the young ones. No danger in misinterpretations there. This we have found to be true. You people fight over books all the time. We want to avoid such conflict.

Joan-Agnes: But how do you transmit important messages to everybody at once?

Darragh: Our important messages are mostly local, which we spread to the community by our sung language. (We do not say 'our spoken language.') Messages that need to be transmitted through long distances are done through our *apollos*. This is a term we borrowed from you. One of your previous gods was named Apollo. Among other things, he was the messenger of the gods. Our *apollos* travel from community to community.

Jim: Where do you come from? Another planet?

There was a burst of twittering wheezes from all around us. It sounded a lot like Celesta's laughter.

Darragh: No, we are terrestrial, just like you. Our favorite human legend of the creation of fairies goes back thousands of years. After Adam and Eve had been expelled from Eden they had numerous children. One day, God came by and asked to see them. Eve brought out the most presentable of them, leaving the puny, sick and deformed ones hidden. But God is never to be fooled. In his anger, he retaliated against the innocent, as he frequently does, and condemned Eve's hidden children to remain hidden forever. This is why we prefer the Scandinavian terms for us, the Huldre, in Icelandic, the Huldufólk, the "hidden people."

Legends are amusing, but they are far from the truth. We evolved, as all earth's creatures did, from common ancestors. We have existed from even before your species did, before creatures split off to form distinct species of insects and reptiles, when we were all still in the oceans. You do not know much about us because we learned quickly to avoid you. We were forced to hide from you. Those of us who did not camouflage well did not survive.

Luna: Where do you come from?

Darragh: We do not even understand that question. We are from here, the Earth. That is the essence.

Luna: I mean, what country do you come from?

Darragh: I myself hatched on the isle of Skye, but I've lived in many places since.

Joan-Agnes: How old are the fairies?

Darragh: We do not keep records of the length of our lives; we do not mark the anniversaries of our lives since it is of no interest to us. We live, that is the essence.

Joan-Agnes: I mean, how old is your kind?

Darragh: Oh, very old, very old. We have followed your investigations into the history of living creatures on earth. We seem to have arrived early. We already had our language even before your species destroyed the other humanoids. You killed off the species that were the closest to you. You are doing it still.

Luna: Why did our cat Gracie not attack Celesta or at least play with her to death?

Darragh: Domesticated animals have had their ferocity bred out of them. We can deal with them, communicate with them. Wild animals keep their ferocity. We understand them, but we cannot be their friends. Some of your domesticated breeds have had the ferocity bred back into them. We stay away from them as we do from wild animals.

Joan-Agnes: Is there such a thing as fairy education?

Darragh: Oh, yes. We teach our young ones our ways of living. But we keep no tally of who learns what when. We all learn at a different pace and that is a fact. No need to fret.

Rick: Do you have gods?

Darragh: This is another question we do not understand. Humans fight to the death over their religions. It makes no sense to us, to kill, to die, over imaginary things. Perhaps it can be said that we worship only what we can see and feel in a physical manner: Nature, the Mother of us all. We love her, protect her, defend her. In return, she nurtures us, gives us life.

Luna: What do you call yourselves?

Darragh: We call ourselves Invisibles. *Tchkl'tsa.* [tʃkl'tsa] That's what we all are. You give us a hundred names: fairies, elves, sprites, sylphs, kelpies, huldre, nymphs, imps, leprechauns, dryads, naiads, nixies, pixies, gnomes, banshees, fays, phoukas, will o' the wisps, shapeshifters, nuggies, spriggans, elementals, numineuses. But we are all one. We look different because when we are young, we decide how we want to hide, camouflaging ourselves as flowers, insects, bark, moss, sprigs, beads of water or dew.

Jim: Well, you truly are Invisibles. There is no sight of any of your friends. Are you sure they're all still there?

At a command from Darragh, there was a sudden outburst of what seemed to be a hundred raspberries from around the garden. We humans found it so comical in its effect that we burst out in laughter. An effervescent cloud of wheezing took hold in the trees and bushes, which made us laugh even harder.

But it was time to speak of serious things.

Rick: Let's go sit down, why don't we?

The four humans sat down on the steps leading up to the front door, Celesta and Darragh settling on the top step so we could see them better.

They looked so alien, and yet so Terran. They looked like they belonged among us. There are weirder-looking creatures in all habitats. A hummingbird-moth and a leaf-covered grasshopper were so natural looking. They did belong in the forest, or what was left of the forest. Unfortunately, not all homeowners provided good habitat for the wild things.

Rick: I imagine that it is very difficult for humans to identify any of you while you are in camouflage mode.

Darragh: This is correct.

Rick: So, the day I "caught" Celesta, she wasn't in camouflage, was she?

Darragh: No, she was not.

Rick: If she had been, I could never have even seen her. If she hadn't been crawling through the leaf litter, I wouldn't have heard her. Had she not been flying around, I wouldn't have seen her.

Darragh: No, you could not have seen or heard her. You thought she was a bird. Some of us prefer mimicry to direct camouflage.

Rick: Celesta let herself be caught, didn't she?

Darragh: Yes, she did.

Rick: Well, why?

Darragh: It was part of our plan. Letting you see just one of us at first was our way of introducing ourselves to you. Humans have a need to know they are in control. Otherwise, you react in irrational ways. As it was, letting you catch one of us was not enough preparation for you humans, was it? You still had a negative reaction when we all showed ourselves to you.

Rick: It is not every day that we see such a sight: hundreds of little buzzing things coming towards us.

Darragh: That is correct. But we thought that having already met one of us and knowing that she was of no harm, well, we thought it was preparation enough.

Rick: Sorry. We should not have been so frightened. Startled, I think, is what it was.

Darragh: We have much experience with humans in this. Humans always have an involuntary reaction to things that they find difficult to explain. They cannot easily accept the mysteries of nature. They either freeze in fear, or they attempt to flee, or they destroy the very thing that frightens them. But whatever they do, whatever first reaction they take, it robs them of the ability to observe calmly and figure out if there is even a threat to begin with. We knew that if you captured one of us first, if you felt that you never lost your predilection of being in control of the situation, you would not have been frightened. As it was, your stress levels were very elevated when you first found Celesta.

Rick: It was the excitement of discovering a little creature I couldn't identify!

Darragh: Imagine if all of us had come out to you that first day. What do you think you would have done?

Rick: I suppose you're right. I would have jumped right out of my skin.

There was a gasp from the Little Hidden Things.

Darragh: Humans cannot do that!

Rick: It's just an expression. I would have been extremely surprised. And probably I would have felt threatened. Even today. Even today, I felt a bit nervous about your great quantity. You are quite numerous. So, I suppose, you are everywhere in nature?

Darragh: We are as numerous as you humans. But unlike you, we know how to live in harmony with nature. We are a part of nature and we view ourselves as being indivisible from nature. You humans enjoy separating yourself from nature. Look at the places where you live! You wall yourself off! You cannot even hear the sound of the rain when you are within your walls!

Rick: You… you… you've been inside my house?

Darragh: Of course, we have. But not even your cats can see us. Why do you think we exist in such large numbers? Because ever since you lived in caves we have been hiding from you. We have known about your destructive behavior for a very long time. Had we not learned how to keep ourselves invisible to human eyes, we also would be creatures on the endangered list! We only make ourselves visible to those humans whom we deem worthy of keeping our confidence.

Rick: Well, thank you… Thank you for that, for your trust. I do miss the sound of rain. With these impact-resistant windows I can't hear much of the outside world. But there are so many hurricanes, the danger… I thought the house needed protection… I… But, tell me, what do you do when there's a hurricane?

Darragh: We hide under the leaf litter, in crevices in rocks, in holes in the tree trunks. You yourself know that in the midst of a hurricane, low to the ground, things are not disturbed. Indeed, that is when all the frogs come out, unafraid of the flying predators, to croak their nuptial hymns. They love getting wet. We Invisibles are not afraid to get wet, as humans are.

There was a sudden whoosh of wheezy laughter coming out of the garden. Suddenly, I recognized the sound. Whenever I had heard it in the past, I always thought it was the breeze in the canopy. Fairies had been laughing around me all the time, but I never knew it. All of a sudden, a thought came to me: Had the fairies been laughing at me?

Luna: So, why did you decide to make yourselves visible to us now? Why us?

Darragh: We need your help. The human destruction of the earth has reached a tipping point. We Invisibles have concluded that we can no longer protect and defend nature by ourselves. We have become visible to you, to those of you we can trust not to harm us or betray us, in the hopes that some humans can join us in the attempt to save nature from your destruction. We have begun to reveal ourselves in every community in the world.

Joan-Agnes: People like the four of us here have been trying to do this very thing all our lives! We are aware that most of humanity is indifferent to the sorry state of the planet, or they place financial profit first, and they either don't care about the harm they do to the environment or they pretend not to care. They just care about taking and taking from the planet and not giving anything back. All they care about is selling wood or fossil fuels or metals, and to hell with the rest.

Darragh: This is why we have come to people who do care, who have shown that they are making an effort to stop the destruction.

Rick: This is why Celesta chose me? I mean, allowed herself to be caught by me?

Darragh: Years ago, we saw you find a dead turkey vulture in your yard. We saw you dig a huge hole to bury it in. Most people despise turkey vultures, but you treated it with respect.

Rick: Well, I couldn't just dump it in the compost pile, could I?

Darragh: You have respect for all life, even those maligned by many people. You have never harmed a squirrel, even though they eat all your sapodillas. You put out bird feed for the wild birds. Your domesticated birds have the strongest, prettiest chicken coop we have ever seen.

How many injured birds have you rescued! Last spring you rescued a whole nestful of baby red cardinals dislodged from their bush. You fed them and kept them warm while waiting for the wildlife rescue people to come. In the meantime, you went out into the garden to get them earthworms to eat! How many people would have taken the time? How many people would have known what to do?

Yes, you do keep domesticated cats in your yard, but you feed them so well they are not interested in capturing birds to eat. We were witness when one of your black cats caught a warbler and you started to run after it, but the cat did not keep the poor bird. It opened its jaws and let it go.

You do not use pesticides on your herbs or fertilizers on your flowers, you use just your compost. You give a big chunk of your harvest of tomatoes and herbs to the caterpillars. The caterpillars provide food for the cardinals but many live to spin themselves a cocoon and burst out as butterflies when they are ready to fly. When we came to this region, all we had to do was follow the butterflies and the hummingbirds, for whatever they like, we like, too. Without knowing it, you provided a perfect habitat for our kind. For these and other reasons, we thank you. We knew we could trust you.

Rick: Why, thank you, Darragh. Thank you very much. I am much pleased to hear you say that.

Darragh: The only human in this region to whom we had ever exposed ourselves was Marjory Stoneman Douglas, a neighbor of yours. We miss her a great deal.

A sudden wail took hold of the fairy hordes. It sounded almost human, except it was so high pitched it seemed to be coming out of human children. The melancholy lament was so intense, it was as if Marjory Stoneman Douglas had died that very morning instead of in 1998.

Rick: You visited Marjory Stoneman Douglas?

Darragh: Indeed we did. We first came to her right after she published her *River of Grass*. We had knowledge that she was a furious defender of nature. Like you, she never killed a spider, not even a centipede or a scorpion.

Rick: She probably thought the same way I did. They were here first. We're the ones living in their habitat.

Darragh: We live in a world where most people are unaware of the wild creatures around them. There is also rampant cruelty. Humans will kill many creatures even before they can identify them. They would rather destroy a thing just in case it turns out to be dangerous. But humans are the most dangerous animals on earth. They seek to destroy, they want to destroy. They hunt for sport. They derive pleasure from depriving another creature of its life. You should see the faces of men as they watch huge forests or grasslands go up in the flames that they lit. Only humans have a lust for destroying. If only they could hear the cries of distress of all the hidden creatures that they destroy as well. But I do not think it would make a difference. Humans are the most selfish animals on earth. They do not even care about other humans. Domination is at the heart of the human soul.

It does not even occur to humans to share nature with all the other creatures. They do not even think of them or their well-being. Why should they: according to them, they have the power to destroy, and their creation myths justify the destruction.

Rick: I feel ashamed for my kind. And angry. Why can't we humans realize that we have ruined the very planet that keeps us alive? With the destruction of the planet, we destroy our own future. An organism cannot outlast its destroyed environment. We're not very *sapiens*, are we?

Darragh: Unfortunately, humans are taking most of the earth's creatures with them as they drive themselves into oblivion. This is why there are many fairies who do not wish to collaborate with humans. They distrust humans and do not want to give them any more chances. Their anger at what men have done to the earth is such that they want to wage war on humans.

Jim: But wouldn't that be a war you fairies would lose? Humans are too powerful.

Darragh wheezed and wheezed in laughter, joined by a chorus of wheezes from his kind.

Darragh: Oh, you humans are so full of yourselves. Your naiveté is breathtaking, as is your arrogance. The Greeks were right: it is your hubris that will eventually lead you to your demise.

Jim: So how could you successfully wage a war against humans?

Darragh: We could have waged war against you numerous times in the past, had we turned to cruelty, to immorality, had we decided to kill the most vulnerable among you. There are stories from your own past that speak of infant snatching and changelings sent to take their place. We know how to make children's milk curdle; we know how to make food disappear. Had we wanted to wage war on humans, we would have already begun. We know the bounty of nature better than humans do. Humans have barely begun to scratch the surface. You have no idea of all the species of plants that can be of use to you, and in the same way, you remain ignorant of many of those species that are harmful to you. We know the properties of plants, we know which plants give hallucinogenic or hypnotic effects, and which contain narcotics, poisons, and toxins.

Had we been as violent, as immoral, as cruel as you, we would have begun to wage war against the most vulnerable of you, the innocent. Just look at your own history! Many of your own wars can serve us as examples.

We live all around you, above you in the trees, beneath the houses where you live. We spend all day and night observing you and we know your weaknesses. We may not understand your inventions, but we certainly know how to disrupt them.

Rick gasps: The TV, the lights, the pool! That was you?

Darragh: Your language is so imprecise! It was not I, yet it was one of us. She did not want to join us in communicating with you, she did not even want us to reveal ourselves to you. Still, everything that she has done to you up to now may be called mischievous, but in no way has it been harmful. If she wished to bring harm to you, she could already have done it numerous times over.

Rick: Who is it?

Darragh: It is my sister, aunt to Celesta.

Rick: Does she have a name?

Darragh: It is Gargora.

Rick: Why is she angry at *me*?

Darragh: First of all, you were holding Celesta hostage.

Rick: But you yourself said that she gave herself up to us.

Darragh: Gargora knew of our plan, but she did not agree with it. She wanted to make her displeasure known. But more than that, she has been angry with you for quite some time.

Rick: Why? What did I ever do to her?

Darragh: It is always what you humans do to us. You are not even aware of the bad things you do to us. You built this house, did you not?

Rick: Yes, I did. What does that have to do with it?

Darragh: Your house crushed many of our living places, including Gargora's. Where her whole family once lived in tranquility, there is now a septic tank. Your pool also dislodged a young couple hoping to start a family. They were forced to move elsewhere. It is true that you yourself are not as bad as most humans. You did not cut down a single oak tree in the yard; you took pains to build your house around the trees, but you had less respect for the shrubs and the vines and the brambles.

Rick: But I replanted with many flowering species that bees and hummingbirds love. I did my best to plant native fruiting trees that birds love.

Darragh: That you did. It is your concern for the living creatures that has brought us to you.

Rick: By the way, how do you even get into my house?

Darragh: Easy as your pie. Some of us can slip in through the cracks beneath doors, through the dryer vents on the roof, down the chimneys. Remember that baby screech owl you once found in your fireplace? If a bird can find its way in by accident, we can find our way in by intention.

Jim: Can you all fly?

Darragh: Yes, we can.

Jim: Can you all swim?

Darragh: Yes, we can.

Jim: Can you breathe underwater?

Darragh: No, we cannot. We have no gills. But we can hold our breath underwater for a very long time.

Joan-Agnes: In folklore, it is written that a good way to ward off fairies is through metal, like putting a knife under your pillow, or hanging bells from the front door, and similar things.

Darragh: You would not stay away from a human with a knife under his pillow? Bells hanging from a door would not hinder you from entering. It is the same for us. The reason why we do not like metal objects is because we know how they are made. Humans cut through the ground, they chisel into mountains, they slash and gash through forests, blast through meadows and glades in order to get at the ore. They pour deadly substances like mercury and cyanide into the ground, in order to force the earth to release its hidden treasures. We are not afraid of metals; we just abhor them.

Jim: But it is with metals that humans began to civilize ourselves.

Darragh: Is that what you call it, *civilizing* yourselves? To us, your simple metal tools led to more complex tools, and the vast majority of those served further to harm the earth. Whereas before you had a hammer and chisel, now you have huge boring machines that do the job so much faster and that are more destructive than ever. Yes, your tools, your machines have made your jobs easier and faster, but the job at which you have been the most successful is in plundering and devastating your home. Our home. The planet belongs to all of us.

Joan-Agnes: Do you mind one more question?

Darragh: Of course not. Your curiosity is one of your most endearing qualities. That is why you like your cats, I suppose.

Joan-Agnes: Ah, yes… why, thank you… Have you ever heard of Oberon?

There was an instant tittering wheeze in the bushes. Darragh was wheezing, too.

Darragh: Yes, of course we have. The "King of the Fairies," humans call him.

Joan-Agnes: Well, what do you remember of him? Do you revere him? Was he a powerful king?

There was a new bout of wheezing laughter that came down from the branches.

Darragh: Humans do not have the imagination to place themselves in the situations of other creatures. Humans constantly attribute their own social behavior to their fellow species. You even attribute your emotions to them. You do this with living creatures and even with inanimate objects. You do it even with your gods. Oberon is as fictitious as your gods.

Joan-Agnes: I'm so disappointed. What you're talking about we call anthropomorphism. We use it and abuse it, at our peril. Bad habit, I guess. But Oberon is still a good story.

Darragh: Your stories, and now your movies, must serve some purpose to your kind, but they deform your attitude towards the other species, cloud your judgment, and interfere with your comprehension of them. They distort your reality. For instance, they have led you to tame wild animals just to be able to call them companions. It would be like us taming the bees or the mantids. Whatever for?

Rick: For precisely that reason, companionship.

Darragh: Be honest with yourselves. You want companionship that can easily be governed, at your convenience. Those poor companions who will not, or cannot, be managed, end up in the pound.

Joan-Agnes: We humans are despicable. We deserve for the planet to get rid of us.

Darragh: Like I said before, your species is taking millions of others with you on your way out. This is the true tragedy. When the suicide opts for offing himself along with innocent others, it is very sad.

Joan-Agnes: Do fairies have to contend with the darker side of their nature? Have fairies been known to harm others, including people?

Darragh: Yes, in self-defense, or in the defense of our own kind, or other creatures when we see they are being threatened.

Joan-Agnes: How do they do this?

Darragh: In ways that are not lethal. We try to distract humans by spoiling their food, making their milk curdle. We create leaks in their plumbing, leaks in their roofs, we clog up sinks and the air conditioning ducts, we hide their keys, we appear only to their children or pets, we make them believe their houses are haunted, we interfere with their sleep, we garble their communications, we move things around to make them think they are losing their memory or their mind. With hunters, we sabotage their firearms, we alert their intended prey. With farmers, we make their chickens get broody so they stop laying eggs, we sow weed seeds in their fields, we cross the wires in their tractors. When things go wrong, humans say that there are "gremlins" on the loose. There are no gremlins, just us.

Rick: Is Gargora going to continue being a nuisance?

Darragh: I am afraid that my sister is one of those imps that give fairies a bad name. Mischief is her true hobby. She does not like humans very much. Why, the rest of us reward people like you who show concern and solicitude for the other species. We reward you with healthy plants, abundant fruits, resplendent flowers. But Gargora believes otherwise. She says that there are no good humans, only extinct ones.

There was a long pause after this revelation. I remember thinking that it would be a calamity if war erupted between humans and fairies. How could humans fight against a foe they couldn't even see? Humans would have to destroy whole forests, savannahs and jungles in order to destroy the fairies. But that would destroy the humans as well. Perhaps Darragh was right and this is apparently what humans do best, prepare the planet for mass murder and suicide. Joan-Agnes changed the subject.

Joan-Agnes: Why doesn't Celesta speak English?

Darragh: Because she is still learning to speak the bird languages. We implement a major portion of our own vocabulary from birds. We also take from reptile and amphibians.

Joan-Agnes: Reptiles have language?

There was another round of wheezing mirth from the trees and bushes. Humans, apparently, were very humorous.

Darragh: Indeed they do. If you could sit still at sunset for five minutes, you would be able to hear the geckos and the lizards singing their bright melodies. As the cardinals cease their frantic love calls, the little reptiles have a window of opportunity. They know the day birds are falling asleep, but the nightjars and owls have not yet come out, so they are not afraid of becoming somebody's snack. They sing while they can. Not as showy as birdsong, but still very pretty. As it gets darker, the frog choruses start and drown them out. Then it is the screech owl's turn to trill his throaty songs. The evenings are filled with the beautiful mystery of communication, but humans are hardly ever outside to hear the concertos. You are all inside, behind windows and screens, in your temperature-controlled bubbles, being entertained by your electronic gadgets. The irony is that some of you watch nature programs, but you neglect the best nature spectacle there is, right outside your home.

Luna: I have a question. One of the messages we understood from Celesta, when we still thought of her as our captive, was that she was on an island.

Darragh: We hiddenfolk prefer to live on islands. It is safer for us to be surrounded by water. Most of us come from northern islands such as Iceland, Ireland, New-foundland. One of the reasons why there are many of us here now is that South Florida is soon to become an island.

Jim and Rick: What?

Darragh: Human tampering with climate is about to bring repercussions that most of you will find appalling. The eastern part of South Florida will become an island, south of Orlando. The east coast of the United States will be submerged between five and eighty kilometers. There will be an inland sea that will encroach onto the land via the Mississippi River. There will—

Jim: How do you know all this?

Darragh: It is too complicated for me to speak about it here and now, but suffice it to say that we are in close contact with those species you call animals. They have been aware for decades that the planet has become warmer. Birds have to travel farther distances when they migrate. Insects from Central America have been crossing the Gulf of Mexico and traveling farther north each year. Some poor creatures have had to move up to higher ground, up the mountains, for cooler temperatures, but when they run out of space they run out of luck. Even here at the local level: have you not noticed that you cannot grow salads anymore, that your mangoes ripen earlier every year, that your deciduous trees are not losing their leaves at all, that your—

Jim: …that our migrating birds go through the area earlier on the way south and come up later on their way back north. Yeah, it's an understatement to say we have been noticing changes.

Luna: Where have you lived before, Darragh?

Darragh: I happened to come into this world in the North, but I had ambitions. As a young nymph I went to France, to Paris, where I stayed for a few seasons. The French do appreciate their flowers, so there was always plenty to enjoy. I stayed mostly in the Bois de Boulogne, in the rose garden. But the reports I heard about Provence sent me there after a while. When I got to Grasse, the capital of perfumes, I thought I was in paradise. It was an artificial paradise, I know, but there was nectar forever. Nature never plants huge fields of the same flower. Once again, humans do things in a peculiar manner for the sake of convenience.

Jim: We call it monoculture.

Darragh: Call it what you will, it is dangerous. The potato blight in Ireland, that is what happened. Planting only one thing starves the ground of nutrients, weakens the plants, which then invites depredation of insects and eradication by disease. That means that pesticides and fungicides have to be used. Once a field is sprayed, we hiddenfolk stay away from it. So do the bees and all the other beneficial insects. It is of no more use to living things.

Joan-Agnes: Where did you live after France?

Darragh: I fell in love with the cananga tree. It has the sweetest nectar, the most fragrant of bouquets. In South Florida you call it the ylang-ylang. Even in Provence it was too cool for the plant, but I first discovered it growing in a private botanical garden near Marseille. By the way, a number of us revealed ourselves to its owner, monsieur de Bonnefoy, and we were his friends until the day he died. He told us many stories of the places where the tree is native, places where it is always warm, never cold, places that never had a word for snow. I went there.

I flew along the Mediterranean coast to Italy, crossed Tuscany, another earthly paradise, across the Adriatic Sea into Yugoslavia.

Jim: It's not called that anymore.

Darragh: Oh, it is not? Well, they had lots of meadows there with lots of wildflowers. After Yugoslavia, then Bulgaria, I entered into countries where there were many arid deserts, but from the locals I always knew where to go.

Jim: You mean, from the local humans?

Darragh: No, no! From the local hiddenfolk. Unlike you, we help each other. You humanfolk would rather kill a newcomer into your community than invite him into your home. We don't do that. We don't understand why you are so hostile to people who come from distant places.

In those desert areas there are hiddenfolk who live there year-round. With their help, I finally arrived in India where I found many, many cananga trees. But they just whetted my appetite. I went farther. I went to Burma—

Jim: It's called Myanmar now.

Darragh: Who can keep up with your changing names! I went as far as Cochinchine.

Jim: Where's that?

Rick: It's what the French colonialists used to call the peninsula where Thailand, Cambodia and Vietnam are.

Darragh: I don't remember a Thailand.

Rick: It was called Siam before.

Darragh: Oh, yes, Siam, I remember.

Jim: Darragh, were you in Vietnam during the war?

Darragh: Which war? You humans have had so many of them! There have been so many of them, I get them confused. I saw human conflict in many lands. This is one of your pastimes. You are always fighting against your own kind. I suppose it is nature's way of culling your species. Humans are the most territorial species on the planet. You cannot abide a people who do not look like you or speak the same language or have the same religion, or some other inconsequential criterion, who live across the valley or on the other side of a mountain. You must evict them, even though there is plenty of space for the both of you. You must have the whole territory to yourself. This creates much conflict and lots of culling. But you have to somehow reduce your numbers.

Jim: Well, what about your own numbers? How do you go about controlling your own numbers?

Darragh: There is no need for that. There is plenty more room for us. The planet has been excessively generous to fairyfolk. There are no starving fairies anywhere in the world. Nature has a profusion of flowers; nectar always abounds. Why, even deserts have their yearly blooms. There is so much sudden bounty that hiddenfolk come visit from far away. These are the places we visit for a week or two, similar to your summer vacations where you go and help ruin other places. We do not ruin; we partake of what nature provides for us and do no damage.

But to get back to the story of my travels, I eventually returned to this side of the earth via Australia and New Zealand, then following the north coast of Antarctica, up Tierra del Fuego and into the Americas. Everywhere I went, I saw humans engaged in conflict between themselves and destruction of their environment. There is no place on earth where humans are not actively involved in the needless destruction of the earth. It is sad and it is criminal. It is time for this to stop.

SATURDAY, APRIL 11, STILL MORNING

We knew that what Darragh had just told us was the truth. Still, we are humans. As humans, we cannot help but have an interest in what happens to our species. We are heavily involved in the destiny of humans, especially those of us who are raising members of the next generation. That last statement from Darragh sounded like a threat. Still, could we afford to get defensive? We didn't even have a convenient riposte. Darragh spoke the truth, and the truth was scary. But now the four of us had been warned, although perhaps it was just informed, that there was another species on earth that was not us, scrutinizing our very unsound guardianship of the earth, judging us harshly, as we well deserved, and in addition voicing a threat against us that it had to stop. There was nothing we could say to Darragh that wouldn't have sounded like blathering apologies—not adequate—or retaliatory indignation—overly defensive. Humanity is guilty as charged. The four of us knew that. I believe this is why the Hiddenfolk chose us to be their confidants. They knew that we would not—could not—invalidate what they were saying. Neither could we contradict their facts with typical human conceit, spewing forth false evidence, distracting declarations or outright lies, which is something that humans do in their sleep. We four were the ideal candidates for the job at hand. We would be the fairies' partners in this endeavor, although we had absolutely no idea what they had in mind to counteract human destruction of the planet. Just thinking that thought put such heaviness in my heart. Talk about Sisyphus pushing his boulder up the hill over and over again! It seemed that success would forever be excluded from our efforts, however honest and strong these might be.

Our conversation ended on Darragh's passionate denunciation of humans as criminals whose crimes had to stop. The four humans slowly went back inside, each of us accompanied by our own thoughts. We were also accompanied by Celesta, who was a comfort in our despair. But as soon as we were back in the kitchen, Luna said something that gave all of us further solace.

"We should find out who the other people are and get in touch with them."

Of course! That was an excellent beginning!

We needed to find out who the other people were, the ones in communities all over the world who were chosen by the fairyfolk to be their confidants. We weren't as alone as we felt! These people were chosen for the same reason we were, so they would also be open-minded, conservationist-type people who agreed with two underlying premises, 1: humans were destructive, and 2: humans needed to be stopped.

This was something we could do. Three of us were highly experienced in social organization. As a professor of French, I had worked in countless committees at school where beans were counted, the reports given to supercilious administrators, and the tree-killing documents piled up high in some godforsaken, spiderwebbed cabinet. But I learned how to assemble the committee members, find out fast who pulled their weight and who dissembled their performance, ignore the shams and get the real work done with the remaining members. Joan-Agnes similarly was a survivor of academe, now retired as was I, and she was adept at workflows, breakdowns of priorities, managing tasks, documenting of progress, sharing information, and providing logistics for the cooperating groups. Jim was a scientist and before that a military person, so he knew how to work in tandem and, more importantly, how to make others work in tandem. Finally, there was Luna, young and inexperienced, but her organizational skills were not to be trifled with. She had basically taken over the organization of my life and it's not easy organizing the life of a self-avowed scatterbrain.

So that evening as we prepared dinner together, Celesta flitting from pot to pan to investigate the progress of the various culinary processes, we took counsel together and came up with a preliminary plan. As soon as we had that settled, we gave Celesta a message to take to Darragh. On a tiny piece of note paper, Luna had written in her elegant script, drastically reduced in size:

Good evening, Darragh. If it is acceptable to you, we would like to have the names and contact numbers of some of the other groups with whom the Huldufólk have been conferring. It is our desire to communicate our concerns with them in the hopes that we can start a conversation that will eventually lead us to find solutions to the deterioration of the planet by human action.

Sincerely,

Luna, Joan-Agnes, Jim & Rick

Twenty-second event:

SUNDAY, APRIL 12, MORNING

By return fairymail we received an overnight dispatch with names, numbers, and addresses of humans chosen by the Huldufólk to be in this impromptu association to which we had also been invited. The list itself was so fairylike it made us wonder at its whimsical fabrication: it was written on long pieces of birchbark with what looked like mulberry ink. The script was diminutive, graceful, and ornate.

As we read the names on the list, tears came to our eyes. The names and the places were so disparate and widely diffused that we had to come to the conclusion that we were well represented throughout the globe. It was a cornucopia of common-sounding names and exotic foreign ones, with Tom and Ben thrown in with Parbati and Aparajita, Pedro and Marcos sharing space with Lü Zhi and Li Quan. The list was very well organized. Each piece of birchbark listed people from different continents. As we perused them, we began to identify names we knew.

Meryl Streep, Al Gore, David Attenborough, Brad Pitt, Bette Midler, Jared Leto, Rachel McAdams, Leonardo DiCaprio, the Pope…

"Why are so many of these people in the entertainment business?" I asked.

"Well," answered Joan-Agnes, who knows more about contemporary American culture than I'll ever know. "These days, guess who passes for influential people? They have the name recognition, the followers, and therefore the means to sway vast swaths of popular opinion."

"Great Zeus!" I exclaimed. "These days you have to entertain people in order to instruct them!"

"That's the way of the world," Joan-Agnes answered. "Have you already forgotten what teaching was like?"

"Yeah, teachers these days have to be actors, psychologists, magicians, clowns, mimes and vaudevillians. Otherwise, the students fall asleep, or worse, ignore you!"

I saw two other names on the list that I recognized.

"Oh, look, Luna!" I called out to her as she made tea on the kitchen island. "Here are people your age! Greta Thunberg and Xiuhtezcatl Martinez."

"Why is Mark Ruffalo in this list?" Jim wanted to know.

Joan-Agnes was quick to respond. "Why shouldn't he be? He's not just an actor and producer, he's also a great person and a political activist. He's got a conscience. I know that he is an animal rights activist and he has long condemned fracking. On top of everything, he is so handsome!"

Joan-Agnes made a smacking noise with her lips as if she were tasting a dainty morsel.

Jim responded, "Still…", then added, "So these are the people the fairyfolk have been appearing to?"

"Supposedly," answered Joan-Agnes. "And confiding in."

Jim followed his line of reasoning. "How in heaven's name is Leo DiCaprio… Brad Pitt!… going to react when they see fairies?"

Joan-Agnes replied matter-of-factly, "The same way we did. With surprise, incredulity, and… well, a bit of fear, I imagine."

"Not Leo or Brad," answered Jim. "You think they'll react with fear? They're not afraid of anything! They'll take one look at those fairies and they'll swat at them as if they were mosquitoes."

"You've been watching too many of their movies," said Joan-Agnes. "Sure, they play roles of tough men, but they're actors and they're paid to do that. Inside, I'm sure they're sensitive, introspective people. They won't swat at the fairies. They'll welcome them into their lives, as we have done. They will understand what the fairies are telling them to do. They will befriend the fairies, as we have!" was her conclusion.

"Look who else is here!" said Jim. "My friend, Arni Finnsson, of Iceland! He's the head of a nature group up there, trying to protect the land from hydropower plants and mining conglomerates." He read from the list. "Iceland Nature Conservation Association. That's the name of his environmental organization. He's a great guy! I met him at a conference in Freysnes, Iceland, a while ago, for National Parks and Outdoor Life and Health, he representing his group and me representing the American Audubon Society."

Luna brought teacups and spoons to the breakfast table.

I turned to Jim. "Sounds like this friend of yours is a much better choice by the fairies to help us out with the task at hand, namely, to put a stop to man's tampering with the planet. What are actors going to do about it?"

Joan-Agnes sputtered her answer in indignation. "They have ideas, too! They're informed. Moreover, they have money. You think the Iceland Nature thing has money? Those institutions have the science, the facts, the statistics, but they don't have the money. You need these entertainers to work in tandem with the science people. I welcome them into our task group. I'll be the one to get in touch with the actors."

"Better you than me," said Jim. "They probably wouldn't even answer me back. I'll contact the scientists."

"Whom shall I contact?" I asked.

Jim said, "You contact the foreign people. I see a bunch of French and Spanish people here."

"But what if they're scientists? Oh, yes, you're a monolingual, Jim. I keep forgetting that. You've been in South Florida so long, I thought some Spanish might have rubbed off on you."

"It has," answered an offended Jim. "*Quiero arroz con pollo, frijoles negros, y maduritos, por favor.* Oh, *con una copa de vino tinto.*"

The three Latinos laughed at Jim's heavy American accent.

"That sounds cute," said Luna.

"I better contact the foreigners, I think," was my decision.

"You betcha," Jim told me. "I'm sure you'll do a heck of a better job, unless you want me to ask them for chicken and rice, black beans and fried plantains. Oh, with a glass of red wine."

"I'll help you with them, Uncle Rick," said Luna. "And I'll also contact Greta and Xiuhtezcatl."

"Great!" I said to them all. "Today is Sunday. I think by Wednesday we should already be getting some responses. We'll convene then, say early evening, after your work, Jim, and after Luna's classes. After, we can have dinner together. *Arroz con pollo, frijoles negros y maduritos* sound good?"

Jim said, "Don't forget the *copa de vino tinto,* brother. Rioja, if you have it."

"Rioja it is," I said.

The plan was agreed to by all.

"But if you guys can stay a while longer today," I continued, "I'd like to invite Darragh over so we can talk more about this sister of his, what's her name?"

"Gargora," answered Joan-Agnes, doing a creditable job with the gutturally trilled mid-syllabic 'r' and the explosively fricative 'r' towards the end.

"Yes, that's it. Gargora. I'd like to find out more about her, and why she's so angry. Angry at me! And why she's always fooling around with my smart-home system. I think I'd like to confront her."

It was Luna who had the final word on the matter.

"It's not enough that you put your house on top of hers? That would have made me fighting mad."

How could anyone respond to that?

Twenty-third event:

That afternoon we had our first April shower. Rain in subtropical South Florida is indicative of the season. The first rains of the year, after our winter dry season, are comparable to the showers up north, and sometimes resemble those of northern Europe: one can walk around without getting wet. But the rain on this day was as heavy as our summer rains, quite out of season, so we decided to meet our fairy friends under the overhang in the patio behind the house. There we would stay dry, but still enjoy the sound and smell of the rain. The smell that the rain brings is heavenly and earthy at the same time. Each drop hits the canopy, or a branch, a blade of grass or a patch of soil, releasing its own scent, and the combination of millions of them becomes a symphony of smells that overwhelm all the other senses save perhaps that of hearing. There is a roar that springs up from everywhere and fills one up with awe. As a kid, I remember taking a book out to the gazebo to read with the accompaniment of the rain. I think I always preferred the rain to whatever book I was reading.

Today's rain was torrential for April. It was due to a tropical wave coming up from the Caribbean. Jim was the first to mention this anomaly.

"Seems like the tropical rains are starting up earlier each year."

Darragh was quick to respond. "You notice your deciduous trees have yet to drop their leaves."

"I know!" exclaimed Jim. They should all be naked by now!"

Darragh and Celesta wheezed their amusement as did a bunch of fairies out in the yard.

Joan-Agnes said to Darragh, "Shouldn't your fairies join us here so they'll be out of the rain?"

"Why would they want to get out of the rain?"

"I don't know,' said Joan-Agnes hesitantly. "So they don't catch cold?"

All the fairies wheezed their laugh.

"We don't catch cold from the rain." said Darragh.

Jim told Joan-Agnes, "That's an old wives' tale. You can't catch a cold from the rain. You catch a cold from a virus."

"I don't know," was her response. "All I have to do is go outside with wet hair or bare feet and I catch a cold!"

"Nonsense," said Jim.

I asked Darragh, "But you fairies don't mind getting wet?"

"We do not get wet!"

As proof, Darragh flew out into the rain, hovered around for a few seconds, then came back to land on my arm. I brought him closer for inspection and saw, indeed, that he was not wet.

"We are naturally water-repellent!" he explained. "Not like you humans who get sopping wet."

"What do you do when you get cold?" asked Luna.

"We huddle together, staying close for warmth. In extreme cold, we vibrate to give off more heat for the others. We keep each other warm."

He began to vibrate his whole body to demonstrate. It let out a faint buzz which had the humans atwitter with amazement.

"That is so cool," said Luna. "I wish we could do that."

Jim said, "Well, we do shiver when our body temperature goes down too much. That's similar, isn't it?"

Luna answered, "Yes, but we don't buzz, do we? I'd like to buzz."

Jim chuckled. "Would your teeth chattering count for anything?"

Humans and fairies laughed or wheezed together. It was so cozy to be enjoying the first big rain of the year together, the humans drinking tea, coffee, or wine, and the fairies sipping honey and maple syrup.

Eventually we came to a lull in the conversation and I took advantage of it to ask Darragh a question that had been bothering me for a while.

"Darragh, I know that you have been around for a long time and you have amassed quite a bit of knowledge and wisdom. Could you please tell me, if you can, why you think mankind wandered away from nature to the point that we lost our way, turned our backs on her, and began to harm her?"

Darragh had been posed on Luna's shoulder. He walked down her arm and onto the center of the table and began to speak.

"You could look to your own philosophers to begin to answer that question. Lucretius, Pliny the Elder, Rousseau, Thoreau, George Perkings Marsh, Michel Serres:[1] They all had an inkling as to why your species pulled away from nature and turned your back on her. It did not happen over a few centuries. It took epochs, eons, for this to occur. I would like to offer you my answer to your question. At the same time, I will be answering the questions as to why we fairies are angry at humanity and why your abuse of nature must stop."

Luna had an immediate answer. "It's because humans have been tampering with nature for so long that we're on the brink of disaster."

"That certainly is part of the answer," was Darragh's reply. "But there is more, and I will include that part in my response to you. Give me a day to organize my thoughts and write them down for you."

"Of course," I said. "And on the subject of fairies being angry at humans…" I hesitated, but even though I hated to make unfounded accusations, I continued. "Am I wrong in assuming that your sister has continued to act like a gremlin? My lights keep flickering, the T.V. comes on, the A/C off, music turns on mysteriously, the pool lights turn on, the sprinklers start to work during the day, the elevator goes up, or down, by itself, I could go on… It's getting worse. What gives? Is it the house that's going haywire? Or is it what I suspect, that your sister cannot stop bothering me? If it is she, I would like it to stop."

Darragh remained quiet and motionless for a few seconds.

"We fairies," he finally answered, "have a code of conduct. I am afraid I will not be able to answer that question until I have conferred with my friends. It is not that I do not wish to answer you, but this is not an answer for me to give. I must seek permission in order to do so to your satisfaction. Please give me more time to consult the others, and I will answer all of your questions."

I agreed. The conversation turned to other subjects while the rain continued and sunset approached.

Before we said good-bye to the fairies, Darragh had one last thing to tell us.

"Please do come to our fairy gathering tonight. The rain should stop once it gets cool. You know the place, I believe. It's the area in front of your house,

1 Please find in the Appendix, section A, a list of the works written by these philosophers.

around the elephant ear plant. We shall be having a dance performance, Celesta being one of the performers, along with her cousin Luzitha and many others."

Celesta twittered her excitement and began to glow.

"It would be our pleasure," continued Darragh, "to have you attend. We will be serving flower nectar, of course, along with pollen cakes and pistil tarts, which I assume you might not find satisfactory to your taste buds or copious enough for your stomachs, so please feel free to bring your own refreshments. The dance shall begin promptly at midnight, but do come whenever you like."

I looked at the others who were beaming me back my own smile. "We will definitely be there," I answered for the group. "Yes! Thank you!"

The fairies all buzzed off and the humans went inside to prepare our dinner. We couldn't believe our luck that we would be witnessing a fairy dance.

Twenty-fourth event:

SUNDAY, APRIL 12 THROUGH MON. APRIL 13, MIDNIGHT TO 4 AM

Staying up past midnight had never been a problem for me. It was the getting up early in the morning that was always my bane. Late into the night, with the rest of the world asleep, in the tranquility of the dark and silence, my mind has always been free to roam and explore, running with the banshee on the moors or exploring grottoes beneath medieval fortresses where Inquisitorial priests cast their instruments of torture into the purifying flames of divine justice.

Jim, on the other hand, was falling asleep on the couch of the media room while we waited for midnight and the fairy show to begin.

Luna, Joan-Agnes and I were excited. I already had an idea as to what went on during a fairy dance, having seen the little lights moving on an elephant ear. But that was from a second-story window through double-laminate shatter-resistant noise-reducing panes; I couldn't hear a thing.

We had already installed four chairs around the elephant ear and prepared our refreshments in advance. I had never known clocks to advance so slowly. But finally, at 11:45 PM, we four humans trooped outside to the staging area. Approaching the giant elephant ear, we saw and heard nothing. I had imagined there would be preparations going on, fairies skittering back and forth, last-minute rehearsals perhaps, but the front yard was still and quiet. There wasn't even a breeze stirring. The leaves were wet from the recent rain and there were millions of little droplets reflecting the house façade lights. I had kept, with Darragh's permission, one of the klieg lights shining directly on the central leaf of the elephant ear. I figured we humans would need help seeing in the dark. The cameras, however, were all gone. We would have to commit this performance to memory.

As we sat down on the four chairs arranged around the stage, we still heard nothing. After the raging rainstorm, nature seemed to have brought our world back to calm and quiet. It wasn't even humid anymore. No wind to stir a leaf.

We waited without even daring to speak to each other. We were as reverential and overawed as if we were inside a majestic gothic cathedral.

One of us had set the timer on a cellphone for midnight. It went off as little chimes that just as quickly were suppressed. There was a huge, instant rustling all around us and above us as unseen multitudes emitted sibilants admonishing us for our unwarranted noise. After a few seconds, silence returned.

A line of lights in perfect formation appeared above us from the canopy. The line descended in unison in a direction perpendicular to the line. In other words, it wasn't a series of lights following a leader, traveling as an arrow, but rather all of the lights came down as a bar, and as it approached the central leaf that was their stage, the bar seemed to sag in the middle, the two ends curving up and by the time they alighted on the leaf they were in the form of a perfect circle. The leaf did not budge when the little lights landed.

Somewhere in our proximity, music sprang up. It seemed to be coming from the bushes around us and the tree branches above us. We knew it to be music, but we could not identify the musical instruments emitting it. We couldn't even be sure they were musical instruments. There were sounds that reminded us of wind instruments, some that sounded like stringed instruments, another one that corresponded to the plucking of a harp. A celestial harp, to be sure. I have in my possession an album of music recorded on the glass armonica, a musical instrument invented by Benjamin Franklin, in which he took the idea of wine glasses filled with water to different levels, each glass denoting a different musical note. To play them, the performer wets his fingertips and rubs them on the edges of the glasses to produce an ethereal sound, as if angels were humming the notes. In his ingenious way, Ben fabricated different sizes of glasses, turned them on their side and placed them on a rotating bar, activated by the performer's foot. In this way, it was the glass that turned, not the performer's finger. All the performer had to do was wet the edges of his fingers and play the notes. The results were a plangent, haunting melody, as if made by the wind itself blowing through crystalline reeds. Such was the fairy music as well, but with so many other levels of sound added to make it pretty well indescribable. In particular, there was the percussion which kept the beat of the music. It was no booming bass drum or even a snare drum. It was lighter, nimbler, something perhaps like the scratch of a match on phosphorus. Then there was a higher-pitched sound, like running a pin down a comb. Interspersed throughout were the sounds like the tinkling of crystal bells. The resulting combination of musical sounds was rhythmic, sprightly, lively. I discovered my foot tapping the ground.

All of a sudden, the voices of a full choir rose up all around us. These were fairy voices, we could tell, because we could recognize the sounds they made in speech, the trills and the clicks and the whistles.

During this time, the circle of little lights remained immobile on the leaf. But when the volume of the music went up, the circle of lights started twirling and then describing the geometric figures I had seen from my window. It was similar to a square dance, only it wasn't limited to eight dancers. I tried to count them but couldn't. They moved too fast. There were at least twenty-five or thirty of them. From my new vantage point, I realized they weren't actually stepping on the leaf. They were hovering above it, fluttering their complicated dance steps as they flew. Still, however, they always kept their dance moves within the confines of the leaf. It should have been difficult to do this because the leaf was not horizontal. The leaf slanted down from the stem holding it up at perhaps fifteen or twenty degrees. And yet, the lights moving in complicated figures always remained equidistant from their stage floor.

Amazing! It was amazing! We were amazed. I looked at the other humans. Joan-Agnes was swaying to the rhythm, Luna was keeping time with her fists, her head tilting back and forth. Jim was still but I could see the look of fascination on his face and his eyes glistened with the tears suspended in them. I felt a feeling like that of being in love. Fascination and curiosity and admiration and a loneliness, a desire to know more, to see more, to be with the object of desire. With butterflies flitting in my stomach, my heart pounding with excitement and delight, I felt alive. I felt so very much alive and energized. I felt I was in love with the fairies, as if from now on I could never be separated from them, that I had to be with them and I knew, I knew so adamantly, that I would help them. I would follow them, take care of them, listen to their every word, and pay attention to them. These tiny creatures were so different from us, so foreign, but they were tons wiser than us. Humans had better pay attention to them. It was to our advantage. As for me, I was drawn into them and convinced of their superiority.

We didn't go to sleep until four in the morning. It was too late for Joan-Agnes and Jim to go home. We just camped out in the media room and went to sleep on the couches. We had a wonderful sleep, our heads filled with dreams of fairyland, of frolicking lights and fabled music, of mythic melodies and enchanting voices. It's as if we had been bewitched by our fairy friends, and even in our sleep we continued to be enthralled.

Twenty-fifth event:

MONDAY, APRIL 13, PREDAWN

The fairy dance with its otherworldly music, its dancing lights moving in sharply-delineated geometric figures, its performers hovering a centimeter above the elephant-ear leaf, must have affected me greatly. It gave me a lucid dream.

I've had lucid dreams often before, and I've had dreams in which I was flying, but this dream in particular was simultaneously wondrous and terrifying. The dream itself was simple: I floated off the couch, ended up outside and flew around. What was unusual about it, and what makes it a lucid dream, was that it felt that I was conscious all the time. I did float off the couch, which was dreamlike enough, but as I rose I could see Jim and Joan-Agnes asleep on their couches, Luna curled up in an armchair with Lucy behind her neck in a position Luna called 'the kitty breadbox,' head erect and all four of her limbs neatly, and invisibly, tucked beneath her. What was not usual was that I dreamt that Lucy had her eyes open and that she stared at me with her celestial-blue eyes as I levitated across the room and out the French doors. I remember the doors were open, that is, I did not go through them as they remained closed. I had the time and the presence of mind to think, who opened them? I also remember feeling the difference in temperature between the air-conditioned media room and the warmer, humid air of the outside. Similarly, I remember being worried that the A/C was escaping through the open doors. I've always hated wasting electricity. My point is, had it been a regular dream, would I have worried about such a mundane, albeit important, matter?

So I ended up outside and I saw my house suddenly getting smaller and smaller and then I recognized my neighborhood, with Sunset Drive, also known as Marjory Stoneman Douglas Drive, to the north, 57th Avenue, or Red Road, to the west, Pinewood Cemetery to the east, and the city of South Miami nestled between Dixie Highway and Davis Road. Then the city lights

became a blur as the vector of my movement ceased to be vertical and became swiftly horizontal. I was flying west at such a frantic speed that in a few seconds there were no more city lights below me. Instead, there was darkness. As my eyes grew accustomed to the dark, I noticed a faint shimmer below me. As I progressed in a westward movement, the shimmer became stronger and I realized what it was. It was the reflection of the stars on the surface of the Everglades. When I turned my vision to the east I could see the dome of light over the city which blotted out the stars directly over it. But here, I could see the stars overhead in their scintillating glory. I could see the Milky Way, which I have seen only a few times in my life, in Tikal, in Colorado, in Banff and Jasper, in northern Scotland. The world had become a resplendent mirror, the profusion of stars above me and a corresponding glimmer of lights below me. It was magical, breathtaking. I could feel the wind on my face. I could hear nothing, except for a faint fluttering sound around me, as if there were insects up here. I looked around but only saw the distant lights of a jet plane suspended in the sky, just like me, towards the north. The plane was in the process of turning around over the Everglades in order to land at the Miami airport. I thought that if there were any passengers looking out in my direction perhaps they would be able to see me. I decided I wanted to fly in the direction of the plane, but I realized then I had no control over the direction of my flight. I was still flying towards the west coast of Florida. I was also still flying higher, I realized, because after a while I could see both coasts of the state at the same time.

The plane had disappeared into the dome of city lights. The Everglades were arranged below me in their nocturnal glory. All of a sudden, I stopped moving. For the first time in my dream, I felt fear. The adrenalin rushed out into my bloodstream and I felt a funny feeling in my stomach and a woozy one in my head.

In previous dreams, it's when I stop flying that I fall down to earth. While I'm still flying, I suppose, I have the impetus of movement that keeps me up, although this doesn't make any sense at all. Gravity never ceases to press its case. But in a dream, reality, or common sense, do quite frequently cease to work. In my experience with dreams, when the forward momentum of flying ceases, my body gives in to the force of attraction to the earth's body and I tumble out of the sky. How many times have I awakened to the horrifying moment I hit the ground, springing up in bed covered in sweat, breathing hard and my heart throbbing out of my chest!

This dream was different. I had stopped moving completely, and I didn't fall. I was hovering, it seemed to me, in a mystical, unexplainable world of a spiritual kind, like a portent that comes to you in a dream. This was a dream I needed to remember. In my dream, I was making an effort to remember the dream. It was during this mind exercise that my sleepflight took on a new meaning, a new direction, and my mind was blown.

I was hovering far above the west coast of Florida, over Ten Thousand Islands, I surmised. I could see the non-reflective surfaces of the islands surrounded by the shimmering water. Due north I could see the smaller light dome over Naples.

The air up here was cool and crisp. It was also light. I felt I had to take deeper breaths to compensate for the lack of oxygen, all the while thinking it pretty cool that this dream was so vivid, so realistic. I felt proud that in the middle of my dream my mind was still paying attention to scientific facts having to do with altitude and atmospheric conditions. Not only was I experiencing a lucid dream, it was also downright rational. Descartes would have been impressed.

But in my wildest dreams, in my most outlandish imaginings, I could never have been ready for what happened next. It would have blown Descartes' mind.

As I floated somewhere above the west coast of Florida, a slash of diamond-sharp light cleft the darkness from the east, beyond the dome of yellowish artificial light denoting the position of Miami. This razor beam of light suffused the sky like a physical wedge, a flat pyramid on its side. The stars overhead dimmed, the waters of the Everglades became swamp water again, but with a metallic patina somewhere between silver and tin, mercury perhaps. This was magic of a different kind. The rays of the rising sun continued to pour their radiance onto the glassy marshes. The domes of light over Miami and Naples disappeared. The world was aglow with a Paleozoic Cambrian sheen, before the advent of higher animal forms. I half expected a meteor from outer space to land on the avatar of this earth that I was seeing for the first time. As the light grew stronger, as I marveled at this primitive planet devoid of any signs of meddlesome humans, my heart beat faster and I found myself breathing hard. It was due to the awe-inspiring sight stretched out below me, earth and sky and water and fire, that ended with the arc of earth's horizon. Beyond that, the flames of the sun rose over the land like an eye just starting to open to observe what had befallen one of its planets. I sighed deeply in my sense of wonderment, wishing this feeling would last more time, yearning for the sight to be burned into my retinas. But my dream ended. Or rather, I don't remember anything else after that. It must have been that after such a strenuous vision, the void of sleep overcame my mind.

Twenty-sixth event:

MONDAY, APRIL 13, LATE MORNING

We woke up late in the morning, hot and sweaty. We had neglected to close the curtains in the media room and the sun was hitting us full on. With the echoes of fairy music still in my ears and the sensation of being light as air in my body, I realized there was something wrong with the air conditioning. I checked the HomeBrainiac display and saw that all the A/C units of the house had been turned off. Furthermore, I heard music, some godawful screeching, thumping, blaring music, metallic rock music, I think it's called, if it could be called music at all. It was coming from the wine room. As soon as I turned it off there, I heard opera—Wagner, I think—coming from the gym. Turning that off, there was a syrupy-sweet, nauseously-repetitive children's song coming from the laundry. From the other side of the house, I turned off a Mexican *ranchera*, a bebop tune and a Broadway anthem, all of which I heartily disliked.

What was this? Something, or someone, was messing around with my smart-home systems again. But this time, they had gone too far. These systems were very sensitive, and very expensive, and if some lowdown fairy freak was meddling with it, he, or she, was going to have to answer to me. The name Gargora snuck into my mind.

After a quick round of coffee and tea, Luna went upstairs and Joan-Agnes and Jim went home to shower and change into fresh clothes. I did the same, expecting the water from the shower to stop at any minute, or maybe the hot water to turn cold. It was a good thing the plumbing wasn't plugged into the smart-home technology.

I was able to finish my shower in peace. But when I went to the sink, I saw the tube of toothpaste lying in its usual place, yet unnaturally flat, completely devoid of toothpaste.

I couldn't wait to get my hands on that little imp, Gargora, that devious pixie, that anti-Tinker Bell, that obnoxious little b—b—banshee!

Twenty-seventh event:

MONDAY, APRIL 13, LATER ON THAT MORNING

The doorbell rang and I was still fuming. But as soon as I opened the front door, my anger dissipated. A flying phalanx of fairies buzzed in the air at the height of my head, holding a rather big object that looked like a book. They flew closer to me and I understood they were presenting me with the object. I splayed both hands, palms up, and they gently deposited the book on them. It felt surprisingly light. The fairies then flew back up in formation the better to see me in the face and clicked and twittered their elemental language. I could feel the little breeze caused by the rapid flapping of their combined wings. The buzzing sound they made reminded me of something, but I didn't have time to dwell on the feeling as the critters flying in formation seemed to be waiting for a response. I blurted out a human, "Thank you!" They reacted with excited wheezes of pleasure and flew off.

I was still all alone, having more coffee. Back in the kitchen, I sat down at the breakfast table, placing the curious object in front of me. As a rudimentary book it was rather ingenious. The edges of the "pages" were sewn together on one side by the "thread" which looked like a natural twine material, probably coir, or coconut fiber, I guessed. The "pages" I recognized as being from my own garden, the papery, leathery sheaths at the base of each culm of one of my bamboo species. The ink was dark purple, again probably mulberry juice like in the list of environmentalists we had received from the fairies.

The top page read: Darragh, Esquire, responds to your Querie, How did Humans isolate themselves fromme Nature, and why they loste their Way.

I wondered when Darragh had found the time to prepare his report, what with the fairy dance having lasted until four in the morning.

This is the full account of Darragh's report:

Sheath 1:
It is tempting to give an
easie answer to these two questionnes:
in a nutshell, you isolated yourselves from
nature, and you loste your way, because you
became too full of yourselves. Too full of your
own importance. It is because deep downe you
are extremelie selfish and you do not care for
the rest of the worlde. As an example, I give you
the creationne mythe in which a vast majoritie of you
believe. The worlde, and everything in it, was created for
you and for you alone. You were even askèd to name the
other creatures. They were yours to do whatever you wishd
with them. God became upset because you ate the fruitt of
a particulaire tree; he did not care that you ate the flesh of
most of those animalls. With them you could do as you pleasd.
And it did please you to do much. By the time you finishèd
manipulating and manhandling the other beings of the earth
you had createt the world's best organizd killing structure; no
spider could have concoctèd a better webbe: from

Sheath 2:
selective breeding to
raising the young, which
you label "livestock,"
in high-density feedlots,
you have taken over what
nature usèd to do. Many
of these creatures never see
the light of day, yet they never
see darkness, either, for artificiall
light is kept on constantly so that they
might eat continuouslie, so that they grow
incessantlie, so that you spend less time and
monnaie on them before you consume them.
And you do consume them, while they are still
young and tendre. Those that you do not eat, you put
in prisonnes around the worlde in order to exhibitt
them and you derive plaisure in their miserie. Your
indifference to the sufferings of other creatures, your
companions on this planett, is woeful when you decide,
for your convenience, to conduct experiments on them.
How would you like it,

Sheath 3:
how would you reacte,
if some powerfull Lorde tooke
your childeren and used them as
subjects of vivisectionne? How would
you stande to see your daughter, your
sonne, your nepheau or your niece, mounted
on a slabbe and see his or her bodie sliced
up from necke to groin without the benefitt of
anasthesia, while the childe was still alive and
awoke, so that the observer could see, for his owne
plaisure and edification the size, placement and
disposition of the organnes in the abdominal cavitie.
Your child would not die immediatelie. It might take
her a few minutes, perhaps halfe an hour, to succumbe
to such treatment. In the meantime, the childe would
feel the handes of the experimenter groping and probing
and pawing through her entrailles. In the ende, the
childe would probablie die of hypothermia; it is difficult
to die from just the paine. The bodie heat of the childe
would quicklie escape from her opened chest and
abdomene, especiallie

Sheath 4:
if the classe room
was aer-conditionned.
Yes, I saie classe room, for
this type of vivisectionne goes on
in hundreds of classe rooms here in
America. You allow your own childeren
to peel open an animall that is alive. What?
For knowledge? For experience that is handes on?
You also teach your childeren that animalls do not
feel paine and do not care that they are dying. Life is
the most precieus thing that any creature on this earth will
protect and defend. Humans, on the contrarie, are the only
animalls that disdaine life and are capable of committing
suicide. No other animall thinks so lightly of life that he or she
will make a decision to ende it prematurelie. Only humans do
that. So, what is it that you teach your childeren? That for the
sake of science it is acceptable to take another life? Because
the life of an animall is disposable, because animalls were put
on this earth for your exclusive use, because an animall cannot
fight back?; humans are stronger and brighter than animalls;
and since animalls are weaker and stupider than humans they
deserve to die?

Sheath 5:

Jim asked me once if we Huldufólk were from another planett. Would that an extraterrestriall race come to this planett and give humanitie their very well-deserved commeuppance! Would that these stronger, brighter aliennes subject humanitie to the same treatment that humanitie has delivered to their own terrestriall cousins! That, indeed, would be justice, justice of the galactic kinde!

But Huldufólk cannot wait for aliennes to come and deliver us from the tyrants. Our deliverence must come fromme within. The planett, by you despoild, maimd, poisond, fould, this orb floating in space, self-containd and indifferent to the egotisticall interests of humanitie, is preparing for your commeuppance. You who think so highly of yourselves, who tout your knowledge and wisdomme, are like an innocent babe, a stupide and clueless childe who is unable to reade fromme the Booke of Nature. You are so keene on reading your own judgements and opinions, so intricately written in your bookes, journalls, and webbe sites, you are so busy fighting amongst

Sheath 6:
yourselves about the
results and conclusionnes of
your mightie scientific straucture,
that the signs from the Booke
of Nature elude you. They passe
right by you unnoticèd, unobservèd,
unmeasurèd, unquantifièd.

You humans have a favorite question you ask
yourselves: "Does a tree falling in the woodes
make a sounde?" Do you knowe how utterlie stupide
this makes you sounde? That you should judge
yourselves the ultimate arbiters of what does or does
not happen in the worlde, that you have such a high
opinion of yourselves, that only you have the meritt,
indeed, the capacitie to describe realitie, is ridiculous.
Humanitie, above all else, is a ridiculous species.

Darragh's tract left me incapable of physical movement. I felt sick, I felt sad, I felt the weight of opprobrium, of insult judiciously leveled at my own kind. Every word, every charge, every incrimination against humanity that Darragh accused us of was true. There was no denying it.

My coffee got cold in its mug as I continued to feel the weight of Darragh's indictment. I felt shame, and guilt. Were the earth to swallow up humanity and bury our tracks forever under stone and sea, it was something we deserved. We had no right to enjoy life on earth even as we trampled, uncaring and unseeing, on everybody else and on Nature herself. Darragh called us a ridiculous species. I knew us to be a destructive species.

Luna came back down for lunch. Joan-Agnes and Jim came round shortly thereafter. They all read Darragh's missive and instantly became introspective.

Luna broke the silence when she said, "Did you notice that no tree was harmed in the fabrication of this book?"

Some of the people we had contacted had begun to email us back. Mostly it was the science folks who, for lack of money or personnel, have to read their emails themselves, without the aid of intermediaries—no secretaries or agents or publicity gurus—to get in their way. From the scientists we learned that regional meetings were being organized in the hopes of coming to a rapid consensus. Politicians were being excluded, all governments shut out because it is a fact that politics always has, and always will, ruin any rational discussion on any topic that involves economics. Politics makes any international agreements impossible. Politicians are always beholden to the moneyed interests for those are what prop them up, buy them up, and keep them up. The scientists warned that politicians should not even be notified that world meetings were being set up. Were they to show up uninvited, they would be shown to the nearest exit. There were, however, a few exceptions being bandied about in the correspondence: Helen Clark of New Zealand, Al Gore of the United States, Wangari Maathai of Kenya, Marina Silva of Brazil, Margot Wallström of the European Union, and Xie Zhenhua of China. Each in their own way had proved that they had the mettle to take on the economic juggernauts and still do the right thing.

So far, the meetings being organized were for the North Atlantic territories, the U.S., Canada and Europe, to be held in Reykjavík, Iceland; for Latin America, in Valparaíso, Chile; for Africa, in Nairobi, Kenya; for the Middle East and the Indian subcontinent, in Goa, India; and for Asia and Australia, in Singapore.

In the hundreds of emails being sent back and forth internationally, not a single one spoke of fairies. I thought that very odd. After all, it was the fairies who were the reason for all this human hubbub. But our own little group of environmentalists in Miami had never mentioned our local fauna of fairies as the catalysts for our behavior. It suddenly dawned on me that for us humans it would have been difficult to admit that a group of fairies were the ones giving humans an ultimatum, forcing us to act. Especially among scientists. Imagine receiving an email: "A cohort of fairies has convinced us of the necessity of ceasing all human behavior detrimental to the planet." The mention of the word 'fairy' would add a touch of whimsy that would make our operations lose all credibility. And think of the criticism we would all receive from the fake-news crowd. I think it was human instinct that censured our communications: we wanted to keep humans at the helm. No fanciful notions of sylphs and sprites directing our activities.

The four of us continued writing emails, forwarding them to others, and replying to all. We still had not heard from a single entertainer, but we were hoping for the best. Luna was ecstatic because both Greta and Xiuhtezcatl had answered her back. Both were planning to go to the Reykjavík convention. The final date was still being negotiated, but we hoped it would be during Luna's break between semesters. She really wanted to come with us.

In the afternoon we took a respite. It was Luna's idea to go outside to invite Darragh in for tea.

"Fairies do no magic," was Darragh's earnest reply. *Fairies do no magic.* The little fairy dressed as a bright-green katydid was insistent on this statement when the four humans had gathered with him for our little four-o'clock tea break, along with Celesta. This time we were all in my library upstairs.

Luna had just asked Darragh what kind of magic fairies did. I had just accused Darragh's fairysister, Gargora, of putting a hex on the house's Home-Brainiac systems.

"Am I right in assuming," I had asked Darragh, "that Gargora has been using her black magic around the house? This morning the A/C was turned off throughout the house and music was blaring from every room!"

"None of it has endangered you in any way—"

"That's not the point! She is still tampering with what is mine!"

"It is tit for tat, if you must know. You are a human; your kind tampers with nature; we take—"

"We've been through all of this before. I'm not one of the bad guys!"

"Each and every one of you is responsible for what your whole species has done. The petroleum industry cracks holes in the planet, pierces her skin, pollutes the air, kills marine life… And yet, you drive a car. You add—"

"It's a hybrid!"

"Were it completely electric…! Where do you think electricity comes from? You think it grows on trees? Well, in a manner of speaking, it did grow on trees. But trees that died eons ago and gave their bodies to the earth where eventually they became coal and oil. In this country of yours, electricity still comes mostly from fossil fuels."

"But I am trying my best. We all are, in this room. We are not the enemy. We are making an effort. Why choose me to tamper with my home? Why use fairy magic to foul up my stuff? It's been Gargora all the time who has been up to this, hasn't it? Well, tell her that she's pissing me off. What kind of sorcery is she using? I won't have it!"

Joan-Agnes interceded, "You're really angry, Rick, maybe we sh—"

"You better believe it! I am beside myself!"

Darragh looked confused for a moment but he continued to explain, "Gargora is very angry, too," he said. "But be aware that she has not damaged you or your house in a permanent way. You need to recognize that it was her home you destroyed when you plunked this house of yours down on it. She still feels rancor and a desire for vengeance. Please forgive her. Everything she has done can be reversed. Had she wanted to bring permanent harm to you, she could have already done so."

Jim spoke up. "What do you mean? What could she do to bring harm to us?"

After a moment of silence Darragh said, "She could have used our knowledge of pharmacognosy."

"What's that?" we all asked in unison.

"For you humans, it is a subject in modern medicine that deals with medications that originate in plants. For us fairies, it is a knowledge as old as plants. Plants are like a myriad of tiny factories that produce so many chemicals that you humans do not know the half of it, actually, the 98% of it. Plants are the source of substances with both beneficial, and harmful, effects. But from the way humanity keeps destroying plants, making them go extinct, you will never discover the usefulness of these substances."

I needed to ask, "So, you're telling me that Gargora could already have poisoned my tea?"

"Indeed, she could have. Many times over. Fairies' knowledge of plant substances is so vastly superior to man's that humans long ago, because of their utter ignorance, attributed magic to their use. A tiny amount of foxglove tea will slow the heart rate; chamomile and linden tea have a soporific effect, but did you know that valerian will put a human to sleep for far longer, long enough to have time to rearrange his books in his study or his spices on the spice rack? Switching the spices in the bottles is even more fun. Changing the roll of toilet paper around is also entertaining. Putting the keys, or the wallet, in the refrigerator is not much fun anymore. Putting them back in the pants' pockets right before they are put into the washing machine is better. Yarrow will keep someone awake for days. Hollyhock, flaxseed and mayapple will keep you tied to the toilet. Belladonna will make you hallucinate…"

Darragh made a circular gesture with one of his upper arms. "I could go on and on. But the important part of what I am saying is that fairies do no magic. Fairies cannot do magic. It would be like saying that fireflies do magic, or that scorpions practice black magic. According to humans, snakes and bats and tarantulas are intrinsically evil and you invent all sorts of stories attributing malevolent forces to them; they are all out to get *you*. But they are all just creatures, doing what they do, trying to survive like all of us do. You humans just do not want to let them do it. Wherein lies the true malevolence? You, by the way, you humans are all just one species, one species that has crowded out all the others. Your species is the one that has cultivated the belief in magic and the belief that there are a chosen few among you who can control that magic and an even fewer few who preside over such magic to the detriment of the rest. You yourselves created the idea of this magic and you use it to intimidate others of your same species and to exterminate them when you need to.

"Why did humans ever hit upon this concept of inventing the idea of magic? It all has to do with your ignorance. Your lack of knowledge. This ignorance of yours is intrinsic and deliberate, because when the creators of science burst forth into your history with answers to age-old mysteries, the vast majority of you continued believing in magic. Look around you at the books on these very shelves! The creators of the scientific method took you from alchemy to chemistry, from astrology to astronomy, from sorcery to medicine, and still many of you wished to go back to your old ways. Magical thinking dies hard. You ignored the scientists at your peril, and you still continue to do so. Worse, here they were, courageous men and women of science doing their mightiest to plug up the holes in your species' colossal ignorance of natural phenomena, and the rest of humanity judged them to be heretics, maligners of tradition, and therefore worthy of being eliminated.

"Ignorant men built entire edifices, whole constructs, based on pure magic. You call it religion. Religion allows you to justify just about anything you want. Nowhere is there religion in nature; you picked it up out of thin air.[2]

"But you also asked me about Gargora. Did she tamper with your house automation system? Yes, she very well did. You see, she is very angry."

"What could she possibly still be angry about?" I asked, probably too loudly. "We're doing everything we can. We've been emailing and calling the other humans. We've been successful in many of these contacts. There have been calls back and forth with some of these people. There is talk of a meeting, a huge meeting with as many of us as can possibly get together. I mean, what more does Gargora want? We're doing everything we can. I don't think we can do this any faster. I mean, there's the time differences, and all. Right now, for instance, I cannot call Europe. They're all asleep!"

"It is Gargora's opinion that man's time is up. There is no more time. Man has squandered everything, the land, the air, the oceans, the other species, everything… even time."

"Well, it's time," I answered, "for me, for us, to meet Gargora." I looked at the others. "She and I need to meet. We must come to a meeting of the minds. Do you agree, Darragh?"

"Yes, if you insist, it must be so. A meeting of the minds sounds reasonable. Just be aware that one of these minds belongs to Gargora. She is our fairy sister and we love her, but… but her mind might take a little bit of getting used to. I shall be present for this meeting of the minds."

"Why is that?" I asked. "Do we need to have you around to protect us?"

"Yes," Darragh answered pragmatically. "Precisely so."

---

2 For the sake of brevity, part of what Darragh said about religion has been excised here. For those who are interested in reading the rest of what he said, please turn to Appendix B.

*W*e all agreed to schedule our powwow with Gargora for this morning. I decided it would be best to gather outside, in the backyard garden, where I have a table and chairs among the flowers. For the humans, we served coffee, tea and scones; for the fairies, we served honey, maple syrup, and agave nectar.

Darragh made the introductions. He and Celesta were quite visible on the glass tabletop, but Gargora was not. The names of the humans had been called out, then the mention of this new fairy we were to meet for the first time, but still we could see nothing. Aware that fairies were perfect practitioners of camouflage, we scrutinized the only place where she could be. There was a flowerpot in the middle of the table where I grew pansies, impatiens, and petunias. We examined every stem and leaf in that flowerpot, to no avail. Suddenly, one of the impatiens grew taller and started to walk. Now that she was moving, we could see Gargora apart from the plants.

"'Tis a feckin' pleasure to meet yous," she said as she took a graceful curtsy low to the soil in the pot.

What a curious figure Gargora cut! She was draped in flowers, multi-colored petals, sepals, with her limbs functioning as their stems. She didn't look at all like a pansy, impatiens, or petunia, but depending on how she moved her limbs and what part of her body she presented to view, she changed shape and color and looked now like a pansy, then as an impatiens, then like a petunia. She even flashed the colors and shape of a marigold and a cockscomb! She could become any flower she chose, just as long as it was on the small side. Her final glorious flash was her pièce de résistance: a drooping fuchsia! She had us spellbound. Luna and Joan-Agnes began to applaud while emitting exclamations of delight. Even Jim was impressed. He had that slack-jawed look of the naturalist who sees one of nature's wonders for the first time. I knew I was supposed to be angry at Gargora, but I admit to admiring her talent. There was no way a human could have identified her as a moving, living, creature. And a talking one, too!

She jumped from the pot to the table and said, " 'Tis always a pleasure to meet the individuals who have grown tired of trashin' the planet and who are now goin' to save it. And who knows, perhaps you'll be savin' your own species to boot!"

"In that order?" asked Joan-Agnes.

"Aye," Gargora replied. "Aye, of course, in that order. The planet comes first. Because without the planet bein' in good health, there is no yous, there is no us. If we fail, the planet will be taken back to the insects and the spiders, and who the hell knows what they will evolve into."

Jim had the next question for Gargora. "With us humans out of the picture, how long before the planet returns to good health?"

"Oh, maybe a matter of months, perhaps a year or two. The climate, that might take a bit longer. Some places, of course, will be contaminated for decades, but creatures will know to avoid those habitats. If yous do not take us fairies into oblivion with yous, we will be able to help the other species and teach them what to avoid, how to act in certain situations. The planet is delicate, but it is resilient. It has been playin' a game with life for eons and eons. Things happen now and then to throw life off kilter for a while, but life clings to this hunk of rock hurtlin' through space with the tenacity of, well… life! There is no other force like it. But yous, whether it has been intentional or not, have been destroyin' huge portions of it, species by species, habitat by habitat. Your destruction has grown as your numbers have grown. You don't even remotely attempt to curb your numbers. You just keep expectin' the planet to keep up with you, so you keep takin' over more habitats, more territory, without a thought to the wholesale death you cause. You're always in need of more and more land, both for your dwellin's and for your agriculture. It does not matter who or what gets in your way. You need it, you take it. No restraint, no awareness that you are oustin' others who have as much right to it as you do. When will you have enough? Never. This is why you must be stopped. Stopped now."

Gargora certainly knew how to cow those humans who were already feeling guilty for our species' wanton destruction of habitat.

"But what of science?" Jim ventured. "You don't think that humans may right their course by the use of science? Science has always gotten us out of jams before."

The little flower fairy changed position to look like a vinca.

"The operative word in your statement is 'us.' Science will help 'us humans' is what you mean. Well, what about the rest of 'us,' the other 'us'? Who will help all of us? Your science? I doubt it. Even yous have problems with your own science. Only scientists feel optimistic when it comes to their science. How often do they really manage to convince the others of their species that their science can halt human intervention in the affairs of nature? Not very often, sadly."

"But knowledge is the first step to making the right decision," asserted Jim. "Science is our best hope!"

"If that is the case," said Gargora, "then I am afraid for this planet and all the creatures on it."

It was spunky little Luna who spoke next. She was nuzzling Celesta who was on her shoulder.

"Why do you not have faith in our science?" she asked.

Gargora walked back to the pot and flew up to sit on its edge. By doing so, she exposed petals on her legs which formed the lilac lip of a cattleya, with both sets of her arms depicting the upper petals as a yellow-green.

"I believe that your science is not up to the task. Even yous have a love-hate relationship with science. Science is your own creation; yous did it by yourselves with no help from anyone or anythin'. Science is your construct, your edifice, but it has not been very edifyin', has it? One would have thought that this creation of yours would have been entirely for your own benefit. Do not get me wrong: just about everythin' in your science has been for your benefit, for your own profit, for your use and your improvement. Better ways to farm, better ways to extract oil from rock, better schemes to make yous masters of all of nature. But science itself, the knowledge it has brought to your attention, has only served to knock your kind off of your position of prominence. You are no longer the be-all, end-all center of eminence. The sun no longer revolves around yous. Neither do the planets or the stars. Yous are no longer the prime receiver of Creation. Yous are just a primate, a simian like many others. Your kind has never gotten over that particular discovery. In a few centuries you have gone from being special to downright common. Everybody now knows that yous are made up of the same material that makes up a worm. Look at yous, proud of your language, your tools, your art and technology, proud that yous think symbolically, use reason, that yous, above all other species, have love, and write sonnets about love. In your mind, your mind is god-like. But science always pulls you back to the ground: Yous are an animal, beholden to your DNA.

"Your evolutionary roots made yous social animals, but what came out of your heads were hierarchies based on arbitrary rationales, such as primogeniture or education or wealth or skin color, which in turn created an underclass and social injustice. Unfortunately for yous, your biology will always remain the same, and all your talents and inventions will be for naught because you will always carry your reptilian brain, and that is what ties you to the animals you so despise. You cannot separate yourselves from your biology. Your mind makes you a god; your body makes you an animal. You are just like the rest of us."

After a moment's hesitation to let the meaning of those words sink in, she added, "All your accumulated knowledge and wisdom cannot help yous. Where does that leave the rest of us? Where does that leave our planet?"

My anger against Gargora had dissipated like dew under the rays of the sun. Her brother Darragh had been saying similar things, but Gargora had a way of speaking that was more forceful, more direct. Added to that was her distracting way of flashing different images of herself. Now she had elongated her body and stretched out her two sets of arms with her opened wings in the background: She was a sunflower, orange, with a dark red center. She was flashy, showy, dramatic. She was fabulous.

After her monologue, we spoke of other things. She already knew about the plans we humans were making, that our world district intended to meet in Iceland. Gargora said that she and Darragh were planning to be there as well.

I eventually brought the conversation to the subject of Gargora playing around with my smart-home system. I knew it was sort of trivial, but it was my home and the tampering bothered me.

"You've been having a bit of fun sabotaging my smart-home technology."

"Well, human, you have put such a temptation in such a convenient package! 'Tis very hard to resist."

"So how have you done it? If you don't use magic, how do you interfere?"

"The same way you do. I use one of the remotes or one of the wall control panels. No harm done. I am no longer upset at you for having destroyed my previous home. It was a very nice home, underground, with solid burrows and cozy chambers. It also had two levels, just like your house. But I barely had time to get out alive when the demolition tractors came to prepare the grounds for your foundation. You need not worry about me now. My new home is behind the little waterfall you installed in your sunken garden. I think it will be safe for me there even when the floods come."

Jim blurted out, "Floods?"

"The floods that humans have unleashed upon yourselves. The whole reason why my kind is even here. You do not know we prefer islands? We come from Ireland and Iceland and Newfoundland. We have known for decades that your tampering with the earth's climate was going to melt the polar ice caps and the glaciers. All of them. There is nothing you can do now to stop the floods from comin'. And they're comin'. South Florida, along its eastern border, will soon be an island. The only surprisin' thing about it is that you are surprised."

Luna said, "Uncle Rick! Celesta… This is what Celesta was trying to tell us that first day. The island. We are going to be an island."

Jim asked, "How long do we have?"

"Not much longer," was Gargora's answer. "But there are still many things yous can do, that yous must do, to avoid further damage. Your own survival as a species is at stake."

Then Gargora turned to me. "My tamperin' with your home was just to keep remindin' you that we are here, and will be here, waitin' for humans to do somethin' about the problems they have created. You need not worry anymore about your smart home. I will no longer tamper with it. Such interference is child's play. Turnin' off your interior climate and losin' your car keys are a lot of fun, but it pales with what is comin'. What is about to happen to your species will be serious, a lot more serious. To us, it will still be child's play. Our favorite games are child's play. To yous, it will seem like the end of the world."

She flew off in a flurry of color and was lost in the canopy.

With his sister gone, the humans looked to Darragh for an answer to this cryptic exit line, but he, with Celesta quickly following, darted off as well. All we humans could do was look at each other's faces and wonder about what Gargora meant.

"To yous, it will seem like the end of the world."

Thirty-first event:

Thursday, April 16 through Wednesday, April 29

After our meeting with the fairies we didn't hear from them again for a while. It was as if they had disappeared from the garden. No sign of them anywhere. I knew they were there, but try as I might, scrutinizing a branch, squinting my eyes at twigs, I couldn't detect a single one.

The fairies' absence gave us plenty of time to turn our attention to the important business of organizing our meetings. The actors and other entertainers had by this time begun to get in contact with the mere mortals. The whole operation was still being done as secretively as possible, so no tweets, no Facebook posts, no loose lips in chat rooms, no instant messaging, no hashtags, no blogging, no WhatsApping or Instagramming or even Snapchatting. But keeping a secret these days is both a virtual and a real impossibility. By Friday, April 18th, there was an online report by MSNBC that preparations were afoot for a worldwide congregation of environmental scientists, along with some supernumeraries chosen for their ability to attract the attention of the media. The report assumed that the meeting was scheduled for one city only, Reykjavík, and didn't name names. The agenda, likewise, was assumed to be about only one item, climate change. As small as the article was, it attracted the attention of critics who loudly proclaimed the hypocrisy that all these people would be flying into Iceland from all over the world, adding a heavy carbon footprint to the effort to reduce carbon emissions. This was a valid criticism. Overnight the proceedings were modified to hold the world meetings online. No one would travel. Everybody would participate from home. This gave rise to the possibility of hackers barging into the summit without invitations. It was the fairies who came up with a wonderful solution. They created an orally expressed code that the legitimate participants would use as a password to gain access to the online conclave. This oral password, in fairy language, would be input by local fairies when the moment arrived to convene. The translation of the message into English was, "Herewith allow entry." Without access to a fairy, an unauthorized cyber trickster would never be able to infiltrate the meetings.

An agenda had been cobbled together and fine-tuned. It was still not finalized, and the members of the different committees would have to attend several of the sections since many of them were so interconnected. For instance, those responsible for "mining" would also have to give their input for the subcommittees on "poisons" and on "habitats," considering that many of the world's mining industries, besides laying waste to the earth itself, were releasing toxins into the environment as well as destroying animal habitats. Some people would be very busy indeed.

The final agenda was released on April 27th. The initial meeting was set for May 1st, adding a symbolic element to the task. May 1st, May Day, as in mayday (abbreviated from the French *Venez m'aider*, come help me), is used as an international radio distress signal for endangered sea vessels and aircraft. Additionally, May 1st is also known as International Workers' Day for all nations since 1886, except for the United States and Canada, which prefer to celebrate its workers on Labor Day, recognized on the first Monday of September. May Day was deemed a good day to begin deliberations. A day traditionally used to recognize the rights of workers throughout the world would now also become known for the recognition of the rights of the planet and all its species. Also, this year May 1st fell on a Friday, and therefore most people would have the day off along with the rest of the weekend. The participants estimated that three full days would make for an excellent beginning to the first serious talks ever about all subjects classified under the heading of environmentalism.

No one anticipated the calamity that would befall humans on the day before deliberations were set to begin. April 30th became the blackest day in the history of humanity.

Thursday, April 30, predawn

Starting in Kiribati, followed closely by New Zealand, then Australia and Papua New Guinea, and so on in a westward rotation as Thursday, April 30th dawned on the world, the terrifying reports began to pour into the internet. By the time that western Australia and South Korea were hit, the dawning world was waking up the rest of the planet's inhabitants with the chilling news. Joan-Agnes has always been a night owl. She was online when the news hit and called me instantly.

She woke me up from a deep sleep.

"Rick, Rick! Get up! Now! Go to Luna's room and check on her!"

"Joan-Agnes? What's happening?"

"I want you to get up right now and go to Luna's room. I need for you to go check on Luna! Now!"

My heart chilled. I ran down the hallway with the phone in my hand. "What's going on? Joan-Agnes, what is it?"

"I'll explain, but right now, check on Luna!" Joan-Agnes was shouting.

I knocked on Luna's door. In spite of Joan-Agnes' alarm, I couldn't just burst into Luna's room. There was no response.

I went in and couldn't see a thing. I switched on the lights. Luna's bed was empty.

"Joan-Agnes? Luna's not in her bed. How'd you—"

"Damn it! Damn it! Rick! The children are gone! The children are missing!"

I was finally wide awake and my heart was beating itself out of my chest.

"Tell me what you know! How'd you know that Luna wasn't here?"

"I didn't know that for sure, Rick. I was just hoping to God that she'd be there. There are reports coming in from the East that children have gone missing. They've suddenly disappeared, from Japan, from Australia, from Indonesia, the Philippines. The kids were in their beds last thing at night—in the morning they weren't. Not the little kids, they're fine. It's the older kids, Rick. It's the older kids who are gone, kidnapped, maybe. The teenagers, they're the ones who have disappeared. Gone! they're just… gone!"

"Maybe Luna is downstairs! I'll go look!"

"Yes, do that! Go look for her! I'm coming right over."

By the time Joan-Agnes arrived, with Jim in the car with her, I had had the time to go into the kitchen, run throughout the rest of the downstairs, rush back upstairs to search in all the rooms, including the library, then back down to check the yard. Luna was nowhere to be seen. She was gone. She had disappeared like the rest of those kids in the East. My God! Was this happening all over the world? I was in the front yard when my friends drove up.

At Joan-Agnes' suggestion we went into the media room to turn on the news. My heart sank when we saw all the news channels reporting on the same story. Children, teenagers were missing all over the world, ages thirteen to twenty. There were images of distraught parents crying and screaming in all languages. Police had been dispatched, but had nowhere to go. In all countries, disheveled prime ministers, presidents, despots, were on the air decrying the calamity, shouting their vituperation, blaming every conceivable possibility: criminals, kidnappers, other countries, the results of alcohol, of drugs, of permissiveness, of lack of discipline in high school education, of indulgent universities, of lax parenting, of loss of the country's moral fiber, the influence of contemporary music, the wantonness of modern culture.

None of it made any sense. Teenagers throughout the whole world had disappeared into thin air. Thin air. I froze. Thin air.

There was something about that expression that rang true, that rang personal. Maybe the kids didn't *disappear* into thin air, maybe they *floated* into it. Maybe they *flew* into it. I remembered the buzzing I heard when I myself flew into thin air. Why would my dream have added such an arbitrarily weird detail as buzzing? Maybe I didn't fly into thin air—maybe I was flown into it.

Joan-Agnes was frenetically changing channels, hoping, I assume, that someone somewhere had an answer to the disappearance of all our young people, Luna included. I told her to calm down and took the T.V. remote from her manic hands, probably one of the remotes used by Gargora in her pranks to confound me. I muted the T.V. Joan-Agnes and Jim looked at me expectantly.

"Just a second," I told them and pushed the button for the internet. I had to type the URL to the website several times before I got it right. The home page of the organization of the environmental colloquium popped up and I scrolled down haphazardly. There it was.

Joan-Agnes and Jim looked up at the big screen. We all read the notice together. It was only a paragraph, first in Esperanto, then in French, then in English, followed by the rest of the languages of the world, all of them.

To the participants of the World Environmental Meetings:

Do not be aggrieved. No harm has come to your children. They are safe and secure and in serene circumstances. They have been temporarily relocated to new quarters where they will be housed and fed and cared for. Those who are found to need medication or medical attention will be immediately returned to their former place of residence. The others will be kept isolated from adults in order to participate in a parallel World Environmental Meeting. It is our observation that the younger generation of humans blames the adults for the disaster that they are to inherit from them. Their solutions will be solicited and compared to and analyzed with your own, with the strategy in mind to take the best results from both world meetings and implement them. Your children will be returned to you at the conclusion of this mutual endeavor.

We looked at each other with fear and worry. This was the fairies' handiwork. Now we knew what Gargora had meant when she said that to us it would seem like the end of the world. But to the fairies, it would still be child's play. Kidnapping our children was child's play to them.

It took me a few seconds to run out the front door. I went to the only place I could think of, the spot right in front of the elephant ear plant.

"Gargora! Gargora! Come here immediately!"

There was no answer, no reaction from the garden, not even a stirring of the foliage.

"Gargora! You have gone way too far this time. Come here and show your goddamned face or I shall cut down every tree in this garden, uproot every bush and destroy all the flowers and burn them. I shall sow poison into the soil and fumigate the garden with toxic clouds of defoliants and pesticides and I shall strip every tree and kill all that flies and crawls. Gargora! You coward! Come here this instant!"

The largest uppermost leaf of the elephant ear was below my fists. I grabbed it in both hands. Fleshy and cool, it seemed sturdy but with the violence of my movement it crumpled and began to shred. I tore and tore until pieces of green tissue flew off until only the thick stem stood upright holding up nothing. It swayed freely now that a weight had been removed from it. I saw the companions, the other leaves, radiating out underneath the forlorn stem. I thought of ripping them up too, but the force of my anger had abated.

Still there was no answer. Jim and Joan-Agnes were with me by now, and we all looked into the darkness of the garden searching for movement and listening for the telltale buzzing of fairy wings.

"Darragh! Darragh! We need to talk, right now! Celesta! Celesta, please. Please come talk to me. How could you have let Gargora do this? How could you have let Gargora take Luna away. We are your friends! How could you let this happen? Darragh! Darragh! Celesta! Celesta!"

I was weeping by this time. Joan-Agnes wrapped her arms around me, as did Jim, and we stood in the darkness of the garden in the middle of the night.

"Why don't they come talk to us?" I asked.

"Maybe… maybe…," said Joan-Agnes between sobs. "Maybe they're not here. Maybe they're with the children."

Thirty-third event:

Thursday, April 30, predawn

Back inside, I explained why the thought had sprung to my mind to search the colloquium website for information about the missing children. I told them about the strange dream I had had.

"I dreamt I floated out of the house and flew so high I could see both coasts of Florida. And when I woke up my shorts and T-shirt were wet."

"Did it rain?" asked Jim.

"It was in a dream!" exclaimed Joan-Agnes.

"Was it?" I asked. "I woke up wet. But it didn't rain in my dream. I think it was the dew. I know it was the fairies. It was the fairies who took me flying. The reason why I was wet was because of the dew, and because it wasn't a dream. I must have passed out because of the high altitude. The air was thin. Which is where the children disappeared into. They disappeared into thin air. In reality, they were transported, every one of them, just like I was, by the fairies."

I could tell that neither Joan-Agnes nor Jim understood what I was saying.

"But why would the fairies do this on the eve of our meetings?" asked Joan-Agnes. "Why would they sabotage the very plan that they had us devise? It doesn't make much sense!"

Joan-Agnes drank water from a glass that trembled in her hand. She put it down on the kitchen counter. "Maybe they did it to show us they mean business. To prove to us that humans need to get serious. Whether it's blackmail or a very sick inducement, they mean for us to come up with results. After all, they're asking the kids for the very same thing."

I glanced at the camera on the kitchen table, still focused on the cage where Celesta had been.

"The camera," I said. "How could I be so stupid!"

I grabbed the laptop and opened it up to the camera app. Joan-Agnes and Jim looked on with great curiosity.

"It'll all be here!" I told them. "If my thing was a dream, we'll find out. Did I fly but it was only in my head, or did the fairies take me out for a spin? If the fairies also took Luna, we'll be able to see right here."

I scrolled back on the feed from the camera in the media room. The camera is placed on a credenza behind the long couch facing the rest of the room, the French doors to the right. I scrolled back to pre-dawn Monday, April 13. It showed images of the four of us, Jim, Joan-Agnes, Luna and me, after we had returned from the fairy dance. We could hear snippets of our conversation as I fast-forwarded the feed.

"Didn't you love it when…"

"How could the dancers keep their distance from each other so precise—"

"Did you notice the percussion? I thought—"

"I noticed a perfume during the recital. It was ylang—"

Finally we were all lying on the couches and armchairs and for about an hour the app didn't detect any movement. At 5:13:48, the French doors opened and a flock, a bevy, a cloud of lights flew in. They went directly for me. I was on the long couch with my head towards the doors. Joan-Agnes was asleep on the other side with her feet almost touching mine. The little lights surrounded me, so I looked as if I had a halo surrounding my whole body. Slowly I rose to about four feet off the couch and then I floated towards the open doors. The camera didn't register any more movements until 6:09:10 when the reverse process occurred. I was brought in by the cloud of lights and set down lightly on the couch. The incandescent swarm left, closing the doors after them. Again, nothing registered on the camera for a while. Finally, at 9:55:32, Jim got up off the couch, followed shortly by Joan-Agnes and Luna.

"You all went into the kitchen. I was last to wake up. I was wet, and hot. Remember? The A/C was off. I thought I was sweating."

"You were pretty pissed, too," remembered Jim.

"And now let's move on to last night's camera feed from the hallway upstairs. It's right outside Luna's room, facing the stairs."

I quickly scanned the feed for the whole night, starting on Wednesday, April 29th with Luna going up the stairs around 11 at night. She could be seen making a left into her room. I appeared on the stairs a few minutes after midnight, so it was already Thursday, April 30th. I made a right to my own bedroom which is at the end of the hall upstairs. The hallway lights turned off at 12:33, followed immediately by the façade lights. After that, there was basically darkness and silence until the phone rang at 2:30 in the morning. That must have been Joan-Agnes' phone call to wake me up. This fact was corroborated when I ran past the camera in my rush to Luna's room.

"They didn't take her out the bedroom door," I said. "They took her out the French doors in her bedroom." I held my head in my hands. "Damn it! Why didn't I install a camera in her bedroom?"

"Because people usually don't install cameras in bedrooms?" suggested Joan-Agnes.

Just then, we heard an alarming sound for such an early hour. It was a distant police siren. It seemed to be coming from the west, from South Miami. In moments we heard a second wail echoing the first, coming from the north in Coconut Grove. Then a third, from the south in Coral Gables. It was eerie to hear the different pitches and the Doppler effects of speeding emergency vehicles. One of them seemed to come down our avenue.

We looked at each other with dread.

"People are waking up to find their children gone," said Joan-Agnes. "Heaven help us."

They're terrorists!

How could they do such a thing! We are their friends!

I thought they were on our side!

They're criminals and they've turned on us!

Traitors! They have deceived us. We trusted them. Now they've taken our children.

Cowards! How can they kidnap innocent children?

This is a declaration of war!

We have to go get our children back!

Screw this meeting! They're not trustworthy!

Who can work with these awful sick things!

They've shown their true colors. Now we must fight against them!

So went the email thread among the participants of the environmental colloquium. Slowly, as the earth turned, they were finding out that the fairies had kidnapped the adolescents of the world. About three quarters of the participants had their own children or their grandchildren or close relatives taken. These were the ones, including me, who were more critical of the fairies, calling them monsters and reprehensible miscreants. The fairies themselves were not in contact any more with any of the environmentalists. All the fairies of the world were missing, too. Their last communiqué had been the post to the website very early that morning. The kids and the fairies had all disappeared together.

"They will be housed and fed and cared for," the notice had stated. We assumed that the fairies were all where the children were. We had no idea how many children had been taken. Some kids were returned almost right away. They were the ones with medical conditions like diabetes, asthma, heart disease, renal failure, anything that required medication, dialysis or daily supervision. The reports that these returned kids gave to their parents, and to the authorities, was that they were taken to places devoid of humans. They told stories of being in forests, in jungles, on beaches, on deserts, high on mesas or mountains, all places that were uninhabited by humans. Those from South Florida said they were in the swamp, on a hardwood hammock, surrounded by sawgrass, palmettos and alligators. Shelters had been provided for the children, built out of natural materials, tree branches for walls, thatch or palm fronds for roofs, straw or pine needles for floors. The huts or shacks were placed around a bigger shelter where the kids could all congregate for food and drink. Their first breakfast consisted of fruits and vegetables, their drink was water and fruit juices, including fruits that they had never before tasted. Drinks were served in real glass glasses, not plastic. As a matter of fact, the kids relayed the information that their kidnap environment was entirely free of plastic. For those in the swamp, citronella candles kept the mosquitoes at bay.

For the children's dessert, honey was served in hollow gourds or coconut shells. Nuts and dried roots soaked in sugar cane syrup, sweet beet marmalade, or sorghum molasses gave the kids the sugar they craved. The obese children were offered the same items, only the nuts and roots were soaked in syrups based on stevia, monk fruit, and canistel. None of the kids complained about the food. Instead, they told their parents that they no longer wished to eat cereals or store-bought cookies or anything of the sort. They had learned that natural food was tastier. That it was healthier for them was something they didn't mention.

The returned kids also reported unanimously that they were not hurt by the fairies, that they didn't see any child being hurt, that on the contrary the fairies were very kind, considerate, and encouraging. They also reported that the last thing they saw before they were whisked back home was the remaining kids sitting down outside and being instructed on how to organize themselves into groups to discuss everything about the environment that they would like to see fixed. Asked if they were scared to be transported by the fairies, the children replied that they had enjoyed it. They couldn't wait to go for another ride.

The fact that kids with medical problems were returned did nothing to quell the ire of the parents. They continued to bombard the fairies with ugly epithets and invective. The more tempered opinions among the environmentalists recommended that the colloquium be allowed to continue. While the authorities looked for their missing children, they themselves could at least proceed with the effort that the kids had also been entrusted with. They must not suspend their discussions on righting the wrongs that man had wrought on the environment. If what the fairies had told them was true, the children would be simultaneously undertaking the same matter, one that was of extreme importance. They should not lose sight of that. But still the more irate adults refused to have anything to do with the fairies, and by extension, with the meetings.

The rational minds continued throughout the day in their attempts to convince the parents. Anger was clouding their minds, they said. It was in their own interest to continue working with the fairies. What they did for the fairies, they also did for humans and for the whole planet. What they still had to do should have been done long ago. The planet wasn't going to fix itself, at least, not while humans were still around.

I for one was convinced. I had been angry, too, when Luna was taken. She was the reason I lived, my treasure, my most precious concern in the world. When I found her gone, my blood boiled and I wanted to take revenge. In my ears still rang the words I had shouted at the fairies, that I was going to cut down all the trees in my garden and mow down the shrubs and obliterate all the flowers. There would be absolutely nothing for the fairies to eat. I realized that those threats, futile as they were, would hurt me just as much. I so enjoyed the peace and tranquility of my garden. It was an oasis of repose and meditation in a noisy, messy world. Fairies and humans were all in this thing together, and humans had just as much at stake, if not more. If we humans were honest, we had to accept a hell of a lot more of the blame for having trashed the planet. I felt ashamed for having wanted to continue the destruction, in my own garden. Talk about cutting off my nose to spite my very own face!

Towards the end of the day, many of the parents had been persuaded to carry on with the discussions. They had a duty to perform, a duty in which they believed wholeheartedly. They would rely on the police to find their children. All emergency responders were called upon to deal with the search. In many areas, the National Guard was summoned to help.

The rest of the world beyond the environmentalist crowd had of course found out about the fairies and their evil deed. Shock and disbelief in the existence of little people soon gave way, for some, to wrath and threats. Most people refused to believe that an entirely unknown creature had orchestrated a worldwide kidnapping of children. But the children were gone. That was undeniable. This criminal act generated a frenzy not seen since the days of the slaughter of the passenger pigeon or of native peoples callously known as aborigines. There arose such a clamor in the land, all calling for retribution. As early as that afternoon, humans with weapons overran city parks, state wilderness areas, and national reserves, hunting for the villains who had dared take their children.

As the environmentalists prepared for their meeting slated to begin on the following day, May Day, they nervously kept an eye on the news. There were thousands of vigilantes running amuck who pledged to bring back the children and mete out God's justice on the felonious fairies. These wackos seemed to think it would be as easy as exterminating rats, which, by the way, as any zoologist will tell you, is an impossible task.

THURSDAY, APRIL 30TH, MID-AFTERNOON

One of the kids who was returned lived in my neighborhood, right on my avenue. Pierre lived up the block from my house, towards Sunset Drive. He and Luna never had play dates together, even though they both had attended Sunset Elementary School, but in different years. He was younger, thirteen, and with such a big difference in age they would not have found much interest in each other. Moreover, Luna never much liked the boys at Sunset Elementary, calling them immature and boorish. But still, the boys were just children. It was the adults supervising them who dropped the ball. Ensconced in a wealthy neighborhood, the school applied a light disciplinary touch on their student population in the effort to ingratiate the parents who, in their turn, coddled their children to such a degree that the kids, especially the boys, tried every day to create their own *Lord of the Flies* scenarios. There was no attempt, not even lip service, to curb bullying at the school. I always tried to imagine what those brats would become one day: cutthroat business executives, unscrupulous criminals, egotistical politicians, or just dead.

Joan-Agnes, Jim and I walked up to the house where Pierre lived. There were so many police and emergency vehicles with lights flashing in front of the house that they spilled over the driveway and onto the lawn.

I knew Pierre's mother, *madame* Córdoba, who was French, married to a Venezuelan man. I had met her at the *Alliance Française* before we even knew we were neighbors. Their són Pierre spoke English, of course, but also French, like his mother, and Spanish, like his father, but neither one very well. His English wasn't so hot, either. Still, it was nice to have polyglot neighbors. We could converse in any of the languages we shared.

Their front door was open. As we walked towards it, *madame* Córdoba saw us from her living room couch and gestured for us to come in. Pierre was sitting next to her, inside his mother's embrace. A medic was removing a blood-pressure cuff from his arm. I introduced Joan-Agnes and Jim to *madame* Córdoba and her son.

"Anne," she said. "Please call me Anne." She had a slight French accent.

"Thank you for letting us see you. I know this is a terrible moment, but Luna has been missing."

"Oh, no!" she cried out. "How old is she?"

"She's nineteen."

"I'm so sorry! Pierre was returned a couple of hours ago. To his bedroom. With all these policemen all over the place and nobody saw a thing. Pierre said he was returned through his window upstairs. From the air he saw people walking around the house, but nobody looked up."

Pierre nodded in agreement.

I continued, "I'm wondering if Pierre could answer some questions for us. We are worried about Luna and want to know if the fairies are taking good care of the children."

"Yes, of course," replied Pierre's mother. "The policemen asked him the same question, but mostly they wanted to know where is the place where they were taken."

I turned to Pierre. "Pierre, did you see Luna among the children?"

"Yeah, she was there, talking to the flying bugs. She was about the only one talking to them."

That sounded to me like Luna, always taking charge of any situation. But the other kids were probably deathly quiet from the shock of discovery that there existed on their earth a society of creatures who could whisk them away to some other place. Luna had had a few weeks' notice.

"Do you remember what they were talking about?" I asked Pierre.

"For sure. Luna was mad, like, really, really mad. She was demanding that us kids be taken back home."

"Who was she talking to?"

"I have no idea. They looked like a flying bug and a flying flower. They, like, buzzed around, talking." He turned to his mother and said, "In English. But I heard them talking Spanish to a bunch of other kids who didn't understand English."

I turned to Jim and Joan-Agnes. "Sounds like Darragh and Gargora."

"You mean you know these creatures?" asked *madame* Córdoba.

"Yes," I replied. "They made themselves known to us a few weeks ago. They want humans to help them clean up the environment."

"Oh, they sound like Democrats!"

Pierre said, "That's what they were talking about!"

"Who, *mon chéri*?"

"The little flying things. They were, like, telling us to get together in groups, to talk about the environment."

"The environment?" asked his mother. "Why would they have chosen that subject as a topic of conversation?"

Joan-Agnes answered the question. "Because humanity has run out of time, according to the fairies. The planet is just about ready to make it impossible for human life to exist."

"The planet?" repeated Anne. "Surely you are making fun! The planet is going to make it unsafe for us? You make it sound as if the planet has its own mind and is planning an attack on us."

I interceded, knowing that Anne's mentality made Joan-Agnes, and Jim, too, angry. Besides, we had no time to explain to Anne that the earth is also an organism, a planet teeming with life, harboring life, etc., etc.

I turned to Pierre. "Did the flying things explain to the children what it was they were supposed to do?"

"Yes," said Pierre. "We were told, not like they asked, to sit around, on the dirt and on tree roots, finding…, like, solutions…, like things we could do to help clean up our environment."

"Were you in Luna's group?"

"No, I was too far from her. I sat down with kids I didn't, like, know. But we didn't know what to talk about. Like, some kid said that they saw nothing wrong with the environment, like, we didn't know what was wrong. If you, like… don't know what's wrong, you don't know how to find solutions. Right?"

"The flying things spoke of finding solutions?"

"Uh-huh, that was their, uhm, their… It was, like, their main, like, thing. They asked us for solutions. Solutions to their problems. But my group couldn't, like, find solutions, because we didn't know what their problems were. We didn't know what was wrong in the first place. We like the environment.

Like, we are for the environment. It's like… you know… the environment's cool and all. It's big. The environment is big and it's beautiful."

He glanced up at his mom who patted him on the head.

"Not like the environment where we were," he continued. "We definitely did not like that environment. That was, like, hot and sweaty and dirty. And we had to sit right on the dirt. There weren't even, like, any chairs around or anything."

"Were the other groups talking about solutions?"

"I don't know, man. They were, like, talking. But I don't know what they were talking about. They were just talking. Laughing and goofing off. But my group, we didn't have anything to talk about. Like I said. We didn't talk about solutions cuz we didn't, like, know the problems."

"That's okay, *chéri*," said his mom. "Do not worry about that now. You are home, safe and sound. That's all that counts."

She turned to us and asked, "Do you have any other questions for Pierre? I want him to go lie down in bed and rest."

"Maybe just one more, if you don't mind?" I said. "Pierre, do you know how long the flying things want to keep the children there? Did they mention any amount of time?"

"They said the kids would be, like, working on solutions at the same time grown-ups were. But when I got home, *maman* didn't know anything about that. *Maman* and *papa* are not working on any solutions. I mean, like, what solutions?"

Jim answered Pierre's question. "Things like, maybe, recycling, or composting, or stopping the production of plastic cold turkey; encouraging society to switch to renewable energy sources, solar energy, tidal energy, wind power, geothermal energy; refusing to use single-use items, banning artificial fertilizers and herbicides—"

"Oh, but please wait a minute," interrupted Anne. "You can't expect children to think about all these things!"

I held my breath.

"Many children already do," was Jim's answer.

But I knew he wasn't finished.

"If enough adults thought about these things, children wouldn't have to."

"You sound just like that girl from Sweden. Greta Thor… Thornberg."

"Greta Thunberg," corrected Joan-Agnes.

"Yes, she's very militant, very dogmatic, radical. She has such an unrealistic perspective. Why do her parents allow her to stand up in front of people, important people, and say the things that she does? Parents are always responsible for what their children do and say, don't you think?"

"We couldn't agree more," I replied. "But what Greta has, more than any other child I know, is a preternatural comprehension of the environmental problems that exist, and a full awareness of the priorities that must be followed if we are to solve these problems."

I stole a quick glance at Pierre to see if he was following any of this. He wasn't. A sudden rogue thought flitted through my mind, of Pierre scratching his ass and then holding his hand to his nose to smell it.

I continued. "But her very best quality is that she completely gets it that we have run out of time. There is no—more—time. Greta has her priorities straight. Any adult who criticizes her should be ashamed of themselves."

Madame Córdoba looked uncomfortable enough. Her last words to us before we got up to leave was, "But why do people worry? The country where my husband comes from, Venezuela, has enough oil for centuries. It's just that the country isn't run well. If it was, there would be enough oil for all the Americas, North America, Central America, South America. But the United States makes sure that Venezuela stays under the foot of a dictator—"

We could hear no more.

"Thank you, Anne, for this opportunity to speak with your son. He has been, like, very helpful. He's a good boy, isn't he?"

"My precious little Pierre has such a wonderful disposition, very *sympathique*, aren't you, *mon doux?*"

She kissed him on top of the head. He dropped his head but was beaming.

"Thank you, Anne, once again."

"Thank you for stopping by. I hope Luna is returned to you quickly."

"Something tells me," I said as I looked at Pierre, "that they're going to hold on to her for as long as they can. But I have faith that the flying bugs are taking good care of our kids. Thank you, Anne."

As we started to walk out of the living room, Jim asked Anne, "Do you recycle here?"

Anne replied, "We did get a recycling bin from the county, and we keep meaning to start. We'll start doing it, yes, for the environment."

We went back home, feeling depressed.

To make us feel more chipper, I said, "I hope they keep Luna and Greta and Xiuhtezcatl for a very long time. The fairies need them, a lot more than they need our kind."

"You mean us adults, don't you?" asked Joan-Agnes.

I looked at her with a meaningful smirk.

Thirty-sixth event:

THURSDAY, APRIL 30TH, EVENING

We found out later that evening that about 40% of the children had already been returned to their homes, safe and sound, most of them speaking of the experience as if it had been a marvelous adventure. Some of them had not wanted to come back so soon. They spoke of it as a huge summer camp in a deserted terrain, with hiking and, where it was possible, swimming, wandering through the woods, slogging through the swamp, rolling down sand dunes, sauntering up mountains, climbing steep cliff faces. It was like a quest, they said, an adventure, a new world to be explored and conquered. Best of all, there were no adults to tell them what to do.

The evening news did not ask why some kids were returned so quickly and others were not. Nobody in the media even formulated the question. But Joan-Agnes, Jim and I, along with everybody else in the environmental colloquium who had the experience of dealing with the fairies, could read between the lines.

Those children who refused to sit in organized groups to talk about the failure of environmentalism were rounded up by the fairies and forthwith expelled from the "summer camps." Those children were more interested in running amuck on pristine settings, whether it be the marsh, the pampas, the steppe, the wilderness, the back country, the deserted island, the bayou, the outback, the glade, or the faraway mountain range. Rather quickly they were surrounded by "noisy pixies" or "squeaking bugs" right before being lifted high into the air and taken back home. We initiates realized that the fairies were fed up with the children who refused to participate in the discussions. Others, we assumed, thinking of Pierre up the block, were returned because they were deemed clueless about environmentalism.

Either way, those of us who knew what was really going on began to call ourselves "Friends of the Fairies," or FoFs for short. We also began to feel much more comfortable about our own missing kids. We knew the fairies were taking good care of them. We felt ready to have our own adult consortium.

But back in the land of the humans, the late-night bulletins brought dark breaking news.

In many countries, the army joined forces with the police to hunt down the fairies. In many of those same countries, including parts of our own, the police itself functions without parameters of discipline, restraint, compunction or even human decency. Similarly, armies the world over have been indoctrinated to annihilate the enemy at whatever cost, with no thought to corollary damage such as civilian casualties. The ensuing union of civil police and national armies led to unintended consequences.

In Argentina, the Minister of Defense publicly clashed with the Minister of Security over the best strategy to use their Federal Police and their military Armed Forces to defeat their children's abductors. Cops and soldiers from the two ministries met by accident in Patagonia and managed to shoot at each other. Twenty were wounded and three soldiers died. The official report blamed friendly fire.

Farther north in the Americas, war erupted between El Salvador and Honduras, each country accusing the other of having kidnapped their children. Thousands of Salvadorans living in Honduras had to flee the violence; thousands of Hondurans living in El Salvador did likewise. Adding to the violence done by the armies, civilians perpetrated rape and murder. Hundreds had already been killed in both countries.

In Hungary, a family of midgets in a traveling circus was attacked by soldiers. The little people had been accused by anonymous sources of abducting children. The two parents and two of their children died; their eldest child, who was of normal height, was spared, but committed suicide soon after.

In Afghanistan, informed that the enemy they were searching for was tiny and capable of flight, the army rampaged throughout the country destroying apiaries, demolishing the beehives, setting them on fire, and roughing up the beekeepers. No children were found, however.

Reports out of Montana and Texas covered sporadic accounts of dwarves and other little people being murdered by highway patrols and private citizens. The killers were easily found: they boasted of having rid the world of leprechauns. Human children would now be safe.

Vigilantes, hooligans, arsonists, and anarchists came out of the woodwork in many countries, taking advantage of the emergency mass movements of policing authorities out of the big cities. While the police scoured outlying areas, the delinquents moved in to riot, vandalize, loot, and burn. Inner cities were ransacked; many suburbs did not escape the violence.

We watched the news with profound despondency. One could always count on humanity to do violence upon itself. The law of the jungle, people called it? That was so wrong. What other species, of the jungle or any other habitat, goes on rampages to destroy for the sake, for the thrill, for the pleasure of destruction? Only man does that. The joy of harm, the rush of ruin, the glee of devastation, man's misery of what life has become for him stirs up a violence that becomes a death wish. Perhaps all the problems that man has created for himself is a craving for punishment, a wish to be eradicated, to be wiped off the face of the earth.

THURSDAY, APRIL 30TH, EVENING

Worldwide, so many drones were released at the same time, both military and civilian, that they started to interfere with airline traffic. More near misses were reported in a two-day period than had been reported in the entire year previous. But drones, as effective as they may be, have severe limitations to the distance they can cover. In the case of looking for the fairies and the children they had kidnapped, they were useless. Satellites were a different story.

The unblinking eyes of the sky never sleep, never fall out of their geo-synchronous orbits. Always alert, always ready, these sentinels are easy to redirect. Thousands of satellites, military, scientific, and civilian, were given new parameters, to scan for signs of new settlements in uninhabited terrain. Using different wavelengths of the electromagnetic spectrum, visible, infrared, thermal infrared, microwave, and others kept secret by the military, satellites scoured the earth looking for signs of new habitations and mass movements of people, small people, children.

But satellites, and more importantly, their human handlers, are trained and directed to look for stuff that is manmade, like concrete buildings, asphalt tarmacs, metal and plastic hangars. No one has been taught to look for palm-thatched huts, bamboo walls, circuitous walkways strewn with straw, and other signs of habitation that are entirely made of natural materials. The eyes in the sky kept scanning back and forth over the very terrain where the fairies had built the temporary shelters. Once the sun went down on that first evening, the infrared sensors on NOAA and NASA satellites, which use Visible Infra-red Imaging Radiometer Suite (VIIRS) instruments, could have been able to pick up the signals of the children's body heat, but those satellites are usually targeted at big things like forest fires or hurricanes. Moreover, the body heat of millions of fairies, since they are indeed endothermic, scattered a million little points of heat over the whole terrain, concealing the heat signals emitted by the children. Ground scatter, they called it.

All of this became moot, however, when the spy satellites began to fail. With the vast majority of them, their cameras simply went off-line. Nothing their operators could do would coerce their birds to respond. With a few of the more expensive satellites, their attitude control systems suddenly came alive. Their thrusters mysteriously came on and propelled the birds to a higher altitude, all the way to the graveyard orbit, where they joined hundreds of decommissioned and expired satellites. With the lifespan of a typical satellite being twenty years, the number of dead satellites has increased steadily, since it takes less energy to push a dead satellite farther away from the earth than to bring it back down to a crash landing, usually in an area of the South Pacific Ocean known as the "spacecraft cemetery." Once the satellites began to move with a life of their own, all the spying ceased. The military has no operational mandates against gremlins. But the NASA and NOAA people guessed correctly: this was the fairies' handiwork and there was nothing they could do until the fairies took their little double-set of hands off of the controls.

Many of these scientists who were themselves participants in the online environmental meetings released this bit of news to the rest of us. I couldn't help thinking that these men of science, as miffed as they were at the interference done to their intricate and wildly expensive equipment, could not but exhibit a grudging sense of admiration and respect for the fairies. The little wondrous beings might look insignificant and defenseless, but they certainly had keen incentive and the intellectual capacity to hobble mankind's greatest triumphs.

Friday, May 1st, morning

By the time Joan-Agnes, Jim and I woke up, the virtual world meetings in Asia, Africa and Europe were well on their way. The participants in North America and South America were just getting ready to plunge in.

We received the reports of items already discussed by our homologues to the East. We were asked to edit the results of their discussions, to approve of their decisions and to express our reservations in case we did not. Easy enough, I suppose. But where humans are involved, complexity arises. Discord usually follows soon thereafter; strife always ensues, hostility and rancor close behind.

For example: Everybody agreed on renewable sources of energy, including wind power. But many people disagreed, and even quarreled, about the placement of wind turbines. They were a hazard to migrating birds who collided with them at night. The response was that domestic cats killed a lot more birds than wind turbines did. Ornithologists at Sibley Guides presented their graph on estimated annual mortality rates of birds that showed that wind turbines were low on the scale. Much more deadly to birds were, in increasing lethality, hunting, communication towers, cars, pesticides, high tension wires, cats and collisions with windows. Joan-Agnes and I let Jim, an ornithologist by study and trade, write down our answer.

"No solution is 100% perfect; there will always be inadequacies, exceptions and unintended consequences in all solutions. But we must look at the bigger picture. While we must avoid putting up wind turbines in known migratory bird corridors, we cannot abandon the idea altogether."

Then there were the obsessives who always seem to crop up in any human endeavor. There were the anti-vaccination people, for instance, who always manage to insert their agenda into any conversation. Here they kept interrupting the discussions by trying to maneuver their argument into a top priority: vaccines, as well as antibiotics, contaminated water supplies everywhere.

They were told that the overwhelming contaminants to water were chemicals caused by fertilizers, pesticides, sewer overflows and wastewater releases, but the obsessives very rarely are willing to see the bigger picture.

It's like the little Dutch boy putting his finger in the dike to plug up a little hole, ignoring the gaping crack a few paces down.

In short, this mutual effort at deciding the priorities of our solutions to improve the health of our environment would turn out to be a long, arduous slog, filled with intermittent recriminations, threats, insults and obstructions.

I wondered how the children were faring in their own colloquium. Something told me that their decisions would be more succinct than the adults'. Theirs would have no parenthetical exceptions to append to their lists of things to do. I knew they would say: "Stop the oil and coal industries dead in their tracks. Train the workers put out of their jobs to work on renewable resources. Jail the executives and the board of trustees for having sacrificed the planet's well-being for the accumulation of lucre. Take the fossil fuel companies' money and put it into research to improve renewables." Perhaps severe, but simple. Also tempting.

Thirty-ninth event:

FRIDAY, MAY 1ST, MORNING

An interesting corollary to our talks was pushed into the agenda by the biologists in our groups. They were adamant that we come up with the proper zoological terminology to denote the existence of the new species, the fairies. Up to now, these little beings had been the creatures of legend, of myth, and like all fictional beings there were wild discrepancies and wacko conjectures about them. No longer. Research papers had already been published in online scientific journals, giving minute physical descriptions of the "types" of fairies that existed in the world. In pre-enlightened times some might have called them "races." But they were all of one species. The reason why they looked so different one from the other was due to the type of camouflage and mimicry they took on. The naming specifications of the International Code of Zoological Nomenclature were followed, and the species name chosen, by popular demand, was *Fata sapiens*.

It was a humbling experience to share the second term of the binomial with another species. *Sapiens*. *Homo sapiens* was no longer the one and only to possess that descriptor. There were many of us who, in view of the intelligence and wisdom that the fairies had shown us, were not sure in retrospect if humans deserved to keep the label *sapiens*. After all, the number of new species being discovered and named every year, around 20,000, was having difficulty keeping up with the number of species going extinct every year, estimated by the Millennium Ecosystem Assessment, involving more than a thousand experts, to be up to 8,700 species a year. In other words, there were many species going extinct that were never even discovered by humans, let alone described and named. Beautiful beings, wondrous creatures, precious lives, were being snuffed out, before we even knew who they were. This loss was accelerating to the point that ecologists were calling it the sixth mass extinction in the history of the earth. This time, however, there was no asteroid impact, no super-volcano eruption, no rapid global cooling. This mass extinction had man's fingerprints all over it. One single species had no right to extinguish so many others. It didn't take much *sapiens* to realize that the guilty species was also going to take itself out.

I would have voted for man's new scientific name to be *Homo idioticus*.

FRIDAY, MAY 1ST, EVENING

The Russians were the first to find one of the fairy settlements. They didn't find it as much as fell on it by accident. We received the report at 6 in the evening, Eastern Standard Time.

At 0800 Vladivostok Time, May 2nd, in the Ulakhan-Chistay mountain range of the Sakha Republic, a troop of Russian servicemen from the Eastern Military District blundered into a fairy village full of children, a few hundred of them. The soldiers had left from the town of Khonuu to explore the protected area of Moma Natural Park in the attempt to find the region's missing children. The fairies had hidden the children inside one of the extinct cinder cones along the Moma River valley. Snow covered the terrain which muffled the footsteps of the band of men. So surprised were the soldiers to encounter the impromptu settlement of huts made of branches and ice, that their immediate reaction was to lay down a line of fire into anything that moved. After a minute of chaos and horror, their commander ordered a halt to the shooting, but not before some of the children lay dead and wounded on the ground, pools and sprays of blood congealing on the snow. There arose a clamor of buzzing and clicking noises from all around the camp, but by this time the soldiers, realizing what they had done, were in no condition to react to it.

Armies were called off in most countries, including the United States, in spite of the direct command of the president who ordered soldiers to continue looking. But after the fiasco in Russia, the American commander in chief lost all credibility with his own military. Soldiers stood down everywhere in the world, except in those places where autocrats still ruled and their warlords followed their every command. In those countries, if armed forces came too close to the fairy settlements, the fairies closed down the proceedings and took every single child back to their home. It was the only way they knew to keep them safe.

SATURDAY, MAY 2ND

It was brilliant of the fairies to divide the FoFs (pronounced "foffs"; Friends of Fairies) into two separate but equal parts. Isolating the kids from the adults accomplished two purposes: it provided an incentive for the adults to get serious and buckle down to business in their colloquia, and it allowed the kids' freshness and optimism to bloom, far away from the older generation's narrow-mindedness and sclerotic ways.

Being away from their parents' influence and pressure also gave license to the children for their frustration and impatience with their elders to boil over, along with their suspicion that many adults would forever be recalcitrant and hypocritical in their weak attempts to save the planet. With the adults it has always been excellent lip service and no action. Their eternal foot-dragging was what had led to their present quandary. The time for moderate steps was long gone. The mindset of the kids was, on the contrary, one of impetuosity and agitation: they were willing to throw the baby out with the bathwater. So what if hundreds of thousands of people lost their jobs with the immediate shutdown of fossil fuel industries? Those people should have known, for decades, that their jobs were as finite as the fossil fuels that sustained them. They had only themselves to blame. The children also blamed the politicians who, always and in all societies, have been peerless at throwing obfuscation into people's eyes as they stuffed money into their own pockets. As a result, the children were merciless in their decisions. Oil fields would be liquidated promptly and turned into nature sanctuaries; refineries and offshore drilling rigs would be dismantled, their materials recycled. The fabrication of vehicles with internal combustion engines would no longer exist as an industry. Not even hybrid vehicles would be tolerated. All-electric vehicles would be the only ones allowed. Superfluous factories would begin to manufacture products more in tune with the Life Economy. The Death Economy would die a sudden and violent death.

Gas stations would close. Oil spills, refinery explosions, offshore drilling rig disasters would all be a thing of the past. The fossil fuel piñata would at last be whacked to pieces and all the goodies inside would be transferred from the politicians to research centers for renewable energy sources.

This is where the children's talents soared. Their imagination, their freedom, their optimism allowed them to create radical new scenarios that would lead to indisputable results. How to clean up the environment in ten easy steps might seem questionable for its naive assumption that society could quickly assimilate and implement its demands, but the children had a formidable protector and partner: the fairies.

No doubt the fairies had been planning this for years, to force the adults to the table by kidnapping their children. Let the older generations and the new one come up with their own solutions in isolation. But the fairies weren't with the geezers. They were with the children, there to defend and protect. Perhaps the kids needed a modicum of supervision as well. But it dawned on us that the fairies were also supporting the children with something else that was indispensable. We, the adults, had the internet with which to communicate. The kids had something even better. The little flying things provided them with a communication network almost as efficient, but with no electronic hardware necessary, no computer, no mail server, no transmission cables or fiber optics, no cell phone towers or communications satellites. Storms in different parts of the world knocked out communications and certain groups of adults were temporarily left in the dark. Not the kids. They were assisted by a fairy network that relied on winged messengers, "apollos," who would be sent numerous times each day to the other kid convocations, which the children called their "powwows," taking and bringing back news of the progress elsewhere. In this manner, a single master kids' agenda began to be built, with the intention that when the discussions ended, the kids' strategy and the adults' counterpart would be compared, consolidated, confirmed, and ultimately configured into the decision-making progress.[3]

The fairies would ensure that the agenda specifications would be followed, to the letter. We were already well aware that they could apply persuasive pressure where it was needed most. It was much more fun when the pressure was

3 Please consult the results of the consolidated agendas in Appendix C.

applied to other people. Even though we didn't have much time to delve online into the news, every once in a while when such a persuasive event occurred, we mailed it back and forth to each other. In North Dakota, Pennsylvania and Texas, solenoid valves, gauges and regulators used in the fracking procedure began to fail, and to make sure that no one thought this was a coincidence, they failed in linked configurations. As soon as one type of equipment was replaced, another one up the line would malfunction. In Washington, D.C., certain emails belonging to certain senators and representatives began to leak as much as the hoses used in fracking. The red-faced politicos would not have wanted the public to see how deep they were in the pockets of the fossil-fuel executives, but fairies give no advance warning. And so it was, in all parts of the globe. We hadn't even finished our talks, but the fairies were already moving on factors that both the children and the adults had conclusively decided: 1) fossil fuels were a thing of the past; 2) national economies would have to be reconfigured to meet this new requirement; and 3) fossil-fuel industry subsidies needed to be redirected to renewable sources of energy.

Time had run out for the Economy of Death that destroys its own resources and nature itself. It was time to embrace the new Economy of Life, the one of constant renewal, the one that will never cease so long as the winds of the globe blow, the sun shines, the rivers flow to the sea, the interior of the earth remains hot, and the ebb and flow of the tides continue their timeless and comforting rhythm.

On this, the third day of our convocation, we received the fairy equivalent of an email from Luna. It was more of an old-fashioned air mail. Similarly, all over the world, adults heard from their loved ones for the first time since their abduction.

Our communiqué arrived in the form of Celesta, accompanied by her cousin Luzitha whom we had first seen as one of the dancers on the night of the magical fairy ball.

They rang the doorbell. Jim, Joan-Agnes and I were in the kitchen where I had dragged my desktop down from my bedroom upstairs. Two laptops were also arrayed on the breakfast table. When we heard the chimes, it was Joan-Agnes who went to the front door. Jim and I burst into a run when we heard her screaming from the front. It turned out to be shrieks of delight.

"Celesta is here! Celesta is here! And she's brought a friend with her! Aren't they the cutest little things you've ever seen in your whole life? How splendid you are! Come in, my little darlings! Come in, come in!"

Celesta and friend hovered in the air in front of us, each holding on to the ends of an object that looked like a long cigarette. Joan-Agnes put out her hands and the two little fairies dropped down onto them. Squealing in glee, Joan-Agnes took them to the kitchen, Jim and I following closely behind.

"Where are you coming from? Why are you here? What are you carrying? Who is your friend?" were the questions Joan-Agnes bombarded them with as she set them down on the table and proceeded to pour honey and maple syrup into small bowls. The two little Fairies put their bundle down and drank their fill. They must have been parched. When done, Celesta stood up to her full height and said, "We have dews of Luda!"

I remembered Joan-Agnes saying that fairy language had no nasal consonants. But we had no idea that Celesta could speak human. We were dumbfounded.

Joan-Agnes was the first to respond. "That is great news, Celesta! It is also wonderful to know you speak English."

"Add Spadish, too!" cried Celesta with pride. "Luzitha add I, we leard hubad speak early. Darragh and Gargora said us start hubad speak very decessary, ibportadt."

Her speech sounded like somebody speaking with a very bad cold.

"Oh, how cute!" answered Joan-Agnes. "You learned human because your elders said it was very necessary and important. You clever little things!"

Joan-Agnes swooped them into her hands and started kissing and nuzzling with them. Jim and I were grateful for the interpretation of what the fairies had said. Never had we been happier to acknowledge Joan-Agnes' experience with foreign languages.

"So this is Luzitha?" she asked.

"She's by cousid."

"She's so beautiful!" gushed Joan-Agnes. "She is so lustrous, so elegant!"

Luzitha was taller than Celesta, a bit broader at the hips, although perhaps that was due to her choice of camouflage. Whereas Celesta had chosen to imitate a creature somewhere between bird and butterfly, Luzitha had chosen to mimic full on a particular species, similar to what Darragh, her uncle had done, who looked just like a katydid. In Luzitha's case, she successfully impersonated a lustrous golden beetle, also called the jewel scarab beetle. She was resplendent in metallic gold from top to bottom. She also seemed shy and didn't say a word although she seemed to bask in Joan-Agnes' praises.

But I was impatient to find out about my niece. "How is Luda?" I asked them. "I mean, Luna?"

"Luda is fine," was the response. "Very busy, but she write you a dote. She write what she add the other childred do." She pointed to the rolled-up note on the table with her dainty little toe.

I picked it up and unrolled it. I recognized Luna's handwriting immediately. It looks French since she learned cursive writing in a French magnet program in elementary school. Students in the English program never learned how to write longhand at all.

Dear Uncle Rick,

I hope you are well and working hard on your end of the discussions. We kids are doing great. We have finished setting up our agenda and are three-quarters through with our recommendations. The fairies allow us to take frequent pauses to relax and eat, and to stroll about. I never knew the Everglades were this beautiful. Especially around sunset. After all this is over, I will definitely want to visit here more often. The sounds at night are mysteriously enchanting and intriguing. So many weird animal calls. It seems the swamp comes alive with all sorts of creatures. But we are not afraid. The fairies never let us out of their sight. Celesta and Luzitha are my constant companions. Fairies really are just like helicopter parents, although the fairies really do hover over us. They are sweet and considerate and make sure we eat well and all that.

They say that they should be bringing us back home tomorrow once we kids finish our discussions.

But it all depends on where you adults are in your deliberations. The fairies say if you need more time, we kids can stay here for another day or two. Do not worry about us. We really are having fun. And I can tell you for a fact that we have been very serious about the work. We have put our hearts and souls into this matter because it is truly something we believe in. It is our future, and the future of the planet, and we are aware that finally something is going to happen, that humans at this particular time will finally do something to rectify the problems we as a species have caused, and that only we together can solve.

I do have something wonderful to tell you: I am no longer afraid of bugs. I look at them and admire them, and I leave them in peace.

I love you,

Luna

P.S.: Hugs to Uncle Jim and Aunt Joan-Agnes.

Forty-third event:

Sunday, May 3rd, morning

Having fairies for company was a great excuse for us to take a short break from our deliberations with our fellow environmentalists. They could wait a bit if their Miami contingency dropped offline for a few minutes. We made a fresh pot of coffee and stuck some English muffins in the oven. Since the breakfast table was seriously encumbered with the paraphernalia of our colloquy, we moved our party to the table outside in the backyard garden. It was a perfect morning, warm but not too humid, and a little overcast to keep the subtropical sun at bay. The breeze rustled the oak leaves and swayed the palm fronds. The world this morning seemed to be at peace, and so were we, knowing that we were contributing a little something to that peace.

Joan-Agnes had brought out butter, cream cheese, and different marmalades for our muffins. One of them was an orange jam with little pieces of orange rind in it. When she offered Celesta and Luzitha a taste they scrunched up their little faces into comical expressions.

"It is sour!" cried Celesta.

Luzitha finally said her first word, "Bitter!", as she backed away from the jar. We laughed.

"But it's sweet, too," explained Joan-Agnes. "Most humans like complicated tastes, sweet with sour, salty with bitter."

"Odly sweet good," explained Celesta. "Sweet give bady edergy."

Joan-Agnes looked down at her abdomen. "Many energy, yes! Sweet also gives a lot of adipose tissue!"

Jim and I laughed but the fairies remained serious.

"What bead adipose tissue?" asked Celesta.

"It means, well, it's another way of saying 'fat.' Sweet may have a lot of energy but it also gives humans a lot of fat."

The two fairies hissed their delight.

"If you fly like us, you have do bore fat. Fly deeds bady edergy."

"Flying needs much energy, yes, I'm sure it does."

I told my story of flying, the time I thought had been a dream. Hovering thousands of feet up in the air, high enough for me to see both coasts of Florida simultaneously, had been a wondrous experience. I would love to experience it again. I would love Joan-Agnes and Jim to experience it, too.

We stayed out for almost an hour. Then it was time to come back in. We had virtual meetings to attend, emails to read, expert opinions to hear, our own suggestions to send out into the ether. Of course we would have preferred to meet face to face with other environmentalists working together for a better future. But the critics had been right. Thousands of people gathering in physical locations would have belied our sincere efforts to lower our carbon footprints. We had to serve as an example to the rest of the world.

As we trooped back into the kitchen, I glanced at my computer on the breakfast table. Its screen was dark so I pushed the space bar to wake the machine up and went to the sink where I placed my dirty cup and saucer. I opened up the dishwasher and noticed its interior light didn't come on. I didn't give it much thought because when the door isn't closed properly, the interior light stays on for half an hour before it turns itself off. But I certainly became puzzled when I went back to my computer and saw that its screen was still dark. I pushed the shift key this time. Nothing happened.

Joan-Agnes and Jim were chatting with Celesta and Luzitha by the kitchen island, talking about using natural materials in which to serve food, instead of china, ceramic and metal.

"I do have wooden salad bowls," I chimed in. "And recently I bought bamboo straws."

The fairies wanted to see them. I went to the china cabinet and produced the artifacts. Celesta and Luzitha approved.

I flipped a light switch to the left of the cabinet. Nothing happened.

"Oh, shit," I said.

Jim asked, "What is it, Rick?"

I flipped the switch on and off several times, to no success. I took a step towards the sink and turned on the garbage disposal. No noise.

I ran back to the breakfast table. My computer screen was still black.

I could have kicked myself. I had brought down my computer from upstairs but I had not brought down its battery back-up. I thought that I wouldn't need it for just a few days. Now we were having a blackout.

"Check your laptops," I said to my friends.

Joan-Agnes and Jim opened up their computers and their screens lit up.

"I'm at 80%," said Jim.

"Mine is at 65%," said Joan-Agnes.

"Check your emails," I instructed.

They did so and found that nothing had been received since a half-hour earlier. That was not normal. We had been getting two or three emails a minute consistently since the world meetings started.

"We're not connected," announced Jim. "There's no connection with the internet."

"Oh, shit," I repeated. "What the hell are we going to do now?"

Forty-fourth event:

SUNDAY, MAY 3RD, LATE MORNING

Joan-Agnes, Jim and I simultaneously turned to our fairy guests, Celesta and Luzitha, who looked as innocent as innocent can be. But we knew better.

Jim spoke first. "Celesta, where is your aunt?"

"Luzitha," I asked. "Where is your mother?"

We knew that Gargora was the cause of this electrical malfunction. We couldn't understand why, however, she would continue to thwart our work. She knew we were serious, and she knew it was we who were trying desperately to find solutions to the planet's environmental breakdown. Why was she ruining our chances? Why did she keep pestering us? Maybe it was in her fairy nature to be pesky and puckish, but now she was being a downright saboteur.

Luzitha answered. Awkwardly and timidly, she said, "By mother with the childred in the Everglades. She dot here. She dot bid here. Fairies dot here dow, just Celesta add be. All fairies with the childred."

Celesta joined her cousin. "This right. Do fairies here dow. Just the two us. Dobody else."

We believed them.

What were we going to do now? We were incommunicado. We tried using our phones, but they weren't working either. We were blind and deaf to the outside world. But I still had a corded landline, I remembered. The only reason why I still had one was because the house alarm was connected through it. I ran to the phone hanging on the wall and dialed the only number I still had memorized, the Tropical Audubon Society House in South Miami. The phone rang and rang but nobody picked up.

"Jim," I said. "Is there no one in your office on Sundays?"

"No, no one's there."

I handed the phone to Joan-Agnes.

"Quick, call someone!"

Joan-Agnes called her sister in Ithaca. She answered right away. It turned out they had no power either in New York State.

Next, Jim called his brother in Boston. Everything there was dark, too.

"Wait," I said. "Let me call a friend in Toulouse."

I dialed the number which I only remembered because it was so easy to memorize. My friend Jean-Pierre answered. He gave us the sad news that there was a power outage in all of Europe. It was late afternoon in France, and soon they would be completely in the dark.

As soon as I had hung up the phone, I turned in a panic to my friends, my human friends and also my fairy friends.

My fairy friends. My fairy flying friends.

I turned to them. Celesta was on the kitchen island. Luzitha was on Joan-Agnes' shoulder.

"My fairy friends," I said. "My beautiful fairy friends."

I placed my palm in front of Celesta and she climbed onto it. I placed my other palm by Joan-Agnes' shoulder and Luzitha hopped up on it. I brought both palms to eye level.

"My magical fairy friends. You must fly. You must fly with all speed right now to tell Darragh and Gargora what has happened. There has been a power blackout here in the United States, at least on the Eastern Seaboard, from what we can tell. And another one in Europe. I suppose that in the middle of the Everglades they can't tell we have no power. Please go to them as swiftly as you can and tell them that our world meetings are at a standstill. We can't communicate any more with our partners."

I took them out of the house through the kitchen door. Once we were outside in the garden, they began to flutter their wings. Before they flew away, they each chose a cheek and gave me a little kiss.

Joan-Agnes, Jim and I watched them fly straight up into the sky and followed them with our gaze until we couldn't see them anymore.

SUNDAY, MAY 3RD, AFTERNOON

It turned out that Darragh and Gargora and, indeed, all the fairies in the world, already knew about the power outages. It was their apollos flying in and out of the children's centers who noticed that something was amiss in the land of the humans. As they flew over populated areas they noticed hundreds of fender-benders at the intersections of their roads. Human neon signs, along with their accompanying buzz, had gone dark and mute. The crackling along power lines had been silenced. In Asia where the sun had already set, the fairy reports coming into the Middle East and into the Eastern European nations confirmed the blackout: it was indeed international, and it was total.

A percentage of the apollos were given special instructions to uncover the reason for the world electrical failure. A fairy with a connection to PowerOutage.us found out that the company itself was in the dark, figuratively and literally. Someone had taken the time to render their generators useless. The humans at PowerOutage tried to pin the blame on the fairies just as we had, but they were quickly convinced otherwise. It is easy to believe fairies. They were an intelligent species who never evolved mendacity or duplicity. Those traits were not needed by fairy society that never functioned under the Darwinian forces of territoriality and exclusion.

Who, then, had pulled the plug on the world? Humans in nations every-where immediately blamed their politicians. Politicians had the international connections to organize and synchronize such an event. They also had sufficient evil intention of putting a halt to the environmental meetings since politicians were beholden to the fossil-fuel energy conglomerates. Humans always like to blame their politicians for any sort of social malfunctions. But fairies had the better conjecture: the vast percentage of politicians are sanctioned and endorsed by the capitalist conglomerates who throw their full weight behind their chosen candidates to get them voted in. The politicians, then, are their marionettes. The fairies went directly after the puppeteers, the company executives.

International conglomerate execs think that they cover their tracks pretty well. But fairies know where they live. All it took was a few visits to certain human habitations before it was found out that the capitalist industrial complex indeed was guilty of coordinating a world-wide disruption of the environmental meetings. True to their sociopathic character, their utter lack of compassion and indifference to human life, the executives were unconcerned about the difficulty and hardship, even loss of life, that followed as a direct consequence of their evil deed.

Social structure is so interwoven with electrical output that humans themselves have no idea how thoroughly they are enmeshed in the web of that particular public utility. The whole world needs electricity and therefore is prepared to pay for it. Once money, lots and lots of money, is incorporated into the equation, the companies who provide that electricity will stop at nothing to keep intact both the flow of cash and their position of power. Ironic now that the power was out: this was a last-ditch effort to hold on to theirs.

We were not kept in the dark for long, although the power was not yet back on. Two hours later, Celesta and Luzitha were back. The fairies had a plan. Of course, with Celesta and Luzitha being such novice speakers of human language, we didn't find out until later all the details. We humans subsequently learned the extent to which the fairies' industriousness and perseverance rose during the crisis. It was decided that, since the kids' meetings were almost over, that most of the apollos would now be diverted to convey the communiqués of the adults' colloquies. Literally overnight, conflicts that had kept the adult groups from forming a consensus, evaporated. Gone were the concerns, the solicitude, the worry about the fossil-fuel company employees. All of those workers, from the crews at offshore drilling rigs, to the engineers overseeing fracking sites, to the poor sap sweeping the floors of the offices at a petroleum refinery, all of them would be disregarded and neglected in the proposed social protection policies. All of those workers were now considered the enemy. They had known for decades the damage they were doing, to the air, to the water, to the land. Every single time there was a disaster, an oil spill, a drilling rig explosion, a refinery conflagration, meager steps were taken to assuage public fears but never to find permanent solutions to the problems. This was no surprise. There were no solutions to the problems. Petroleum extraction and implementation is a danger to living things at every step of the way. The danger has ramifications that project it into the interference and tampering with every natural element and all animal habitats.

The fossil fuel industries thought that by throwing the world into the dark they would bring it to its knees. Their strategy backfired spectacularly. It stripped every final vestige of sympathy the environmentalists may have held for the workers who would be thrown out of work. The enviros now knew that sacrifices had to be made, social sacrifices as well as personal ones. Those enviros who still had vehicles that used internal combustion engines knew their cars would be worthless—and useless—after their meetings had concluded. From now on, they would treat human society, as hooked as it was to fossil fuels and as dependent as it was on substances with deleterious effects, as the addict who needs to quit cold turkey. The fossil fuel industries were the drug pusher addicted to profits, ramming oil and gas and coal down the throat of humankind. They had to go. All of them. Immediately.

But at the moment of Celesta and Luzitha's arrival, they communicated just enough to let us know that the fairy apollos would now be carrying messages to our colleagues and bringing back their responses. This is how we met Quercus and Abiès who flew down the chimney into the music room. Joan-Agnes, Jim and I were huddled together with our two little girl fairies at the kitchen table when suddenly the two little bloke fairies swooped in. We weren't quite ready for the likes of them.

Forty-sixth event:

SUNDAY, MAY 3RD, AFTERNOON THROUGH FRIDAY, MAY 15TH

Quercus and Abiès were fleet flyers who took both their names and disguises from different genera of trees. Quercus looked like a sprig of oak leaves, including a couple of acorns hanging from the sides of his head. He looked like he was wearing oversized earrings. Abiès looked like a branchlet off a white fir, spiky with its telltale broad needles. He had a couple of miniature pine cones growing on his upper back. As always, we humans were amazed at the efficacy of fairy camouflage.

We found out that Quercus and Abiès were cousins and that their fathers came from a long line of tree camouflagers. Quercus' father, Acer, mimicked a Bigleaf maple and had the added talent of changing the colors of his 'leaves' in the fall. During the winter he went around looking like a naked twig. Acer's brother, Piceagh, imitated a Blue Spruce. In the winter he would affix white moss on his 'branches' which he would then carry lower as if they were encumbered with snow.

The newcomers' dominion of the English language was excellent. They were able to fill us in on a lot of details about what was happening out in the world. Enviros everywhere were reaching out to those humans involved in the renewable energy companies. Something that had been projected into the future was now being worked on in urgency: how to wean the production of electricity off fossil fuels and reattach them to renewable energy sources. With so many minds, so much expertise, so much knowledge that existed already, inroads were being made apace throughout the world.

For years, the scientists working on solar, wind, hydro, biomass and geothermal renewable energy sources had been stymied by the combined forces of the fossil fuel companies and the politicians in their pockets. Suddenly, in one fell swoop, this monolithic impediment was broken. Once the truth was out that the fossil fuel fiends were responsible for the outages, there was an outcry from the public to get rid of them, even to bring them to trial. In one stupid move, the fossil fuel idiots made themselves obsolete and expendable. The renewable energy sources people had been trying for decades to jockey into position and now, today, they had their chance to shine.

Our colloquies took on a new priority, to help the experts combine their forces and develop and consolidate a network that would replace the burning of oil, gas, and coal to produce the energy that society needed. No one was naive enough to think we could do this in a few days. We knew we could not replace the old system all at once, but we were willing to make the effort. There was no other choice. We would all have to make sacrifices.

But one of them wasn't with our communications systems. The fairy apollos were taking care of that. We no longer had the instantaneousness of emails, but with the apollos working in relays we could transmit a message to Europe within a day. This is how we found out that Iceland was the first nation to divert its power generation completely to geothermal sources. The nine tidal power plants already built and functioning throughout the world were able to provide enough megawatts for hospitals and other emergency service providers. Similarly, the fifty-eight fully functional solar power plants in the world and the too-numerous to mention wind turbines and biomass power plants provided their regions with sorely needed energy. It was still only a tiny fraction of the power supply the world had produced before the Big Dark. But it was a start. It also served to prove to the fossil fuel extortionists that their heyday was over. And when the fairies came up with a list of the names of the evil organizers of the world blackout, complete with their home addresses and telephone numbers, the fossil fuel malefactors, now themselves fossils of an earlier age, were arrested and dealt with according to the laws of the nations in which they lived. Slowly in the days that followed, the lights began to turn back on all over the world.

TUESDAY, MAY 5TH

Our children were brought back to us today. It was a joyous day, full of exhilaration and thanksgiving and hope.

With no A/C, our windows were wide open. Joan-Agnes, Jim and I heard the twittering hiccups of the fairies announcing their arrival and we rushed out the kitchen door to the back yard. There they were, flashing and zipping around in colorful and boisterous darts and flits. For a secretive and guarded species, they could certainly put up quite a din when they wanted to. We saw them looking up. We followed their gaze and saw Luna descending from the heavens. The sun behind her made her seem like she was enveloped in a halo. As soon as her fairy pilots set her down on the lawn we were all over her, kissing and hugging her and crying fat tears. The fairies surrounded us with a boundless cloud of euphoria, of deliverance and protection. Luna could not contain her ebullience, talking excitedly and embracing us in turn, then turning to the cloud of fairy well-wishers. Luna held up her hands to signify she wished to speak. The human and fairy clamor ceased. Luna looked around her, her eyes brimming with tears. The fairies hovered in place, motionless save for the blur of their wings.

"To say that you, good and kind fairies, have helped us, well, that is not enough. To say that your concern and devotion to nature have brought us humans back from the brink is not enough. To say that you have saved us—that you even thought we were worth saving in the first place—by your passion and your perseverance, is not enough. To say that you have saved the entire planet is still not enough. You may be little, tiny even, but in the past few days you have moved mountains. You have moved us from our indifference and scorn to the realization that we belong in nature and that we are vested in her because we are not separate from her. You have opened our eyes. You have made us see that we are not alone. We have never been alone. Nature envelops us and we are part of her. She is our planet, our home—we have no other. You helped us see how wrong we were, how destructive we were. You helped us to understand that the world is not infinite, and that by our carelessness and our destructive bloodlust we have been killing our fellow creatures, to our detriment.

"The birds in the sky, we are told, 'they do not sow, neither do they reap,' and yet they die by the multitudes by our actions. Look at the lilies of the field: 'they do not toil, neither do they spin,' yet they have shriveled to dust. The naked fields have been hollowed out by the winds and lie barren and tainted. How can we—how dare we—judge that we are better than the birds of the sky or the lilies of the field? How could we ever think that we are of more value than they? All this time we have been blinded, we have been duped by our own myths that we created out of our own sense of self-importance. Our naive and self-serving legends have perpetuated our belief that we were put on earth to be masters of all creation, that we have dominion over all the other species. You are small, but you are intelligent. You have made us understand that our notions of our place of privilege and supremacy should have gone away with the idea that the sun and the moon and the stars all revolve around us. We are not superior; we prove this every day by our very violence and our indifference to the consequences of our violence. Nature herself is violent and she is also indifferent, but that does not give us the right to fight against her. Humans think we can separate ourselves from Nature, but we cannot, and we cannot kill her and her creatures without killing a part of ourselves, or killing ourselves outright. You have made us understand this. Nothing we can say, no words of thanks we can pronounce, will ever be enough to show our gratitude to you, my beautiful flying fairies. With your wisdom and your love, you have taught us how to heal the world, and how to heal ourselves."

There was an uproar of clicks, whistles and chittering from all around us. Darragh and Gargora both flew down and embraced Luna's earlobes and Celesta and Luzitha danced on her shoulders. Joan-Agnes, Jim and I began a dance of our own around Luna. We might as well have been in a forest glade dancing the dance of the ancient Druids, of pantheists who believed that the manifestation of deities permeated all of Nature, whose name was Gaia; the planet was worthy of being protected, and we were her protectors, fairies first, with us humans following, belatedly, but still following.

Luna laughed with joy. She had three loving humans around her and hundreds of fairies above her.

"This is my niece!" I shouted.

I could not have been more proud of her as I was at that instant.

TUESDAY, MAY 5TH AND INTO THE FUTURE

Luna was back, as were most of our garden fairies. Only Quercus and Abiès were missing, along with the other apollos who were still busy flitting from place to place, solemnly and speedily fulfilling their duty as messengers to the human colloquies. Joan-Agnes, Jim and I could now thoroughly give ourselves over to the jubilation we felt at having Luna back. We still didn't have power back in South Florida, nor were we expecting it soon. But hope, which we had utterly lacked before, was now a constant companion. We knew that our state, our whole country, had had a poor track record of allowing renewables to attach themselves to the energy grid. We knew that we lagged far behind other countries. Paying the piper had never been so difficult and yet so satisfying. We had hated for decades the fossil fuel monopolies for the damage that their extraction from the earth caused. It was a huge weight off our shoulders, to say nothing of the earth's, to witness the day that humanity weaned itself off their destructiveness.

The sacrifices we yet had to make were extreme. Here in South Florida, our situation was worse than the aftermath of the strongest hurricanes. With the stoppage of the fossil fuel industry, the transport of food came to a sudden halt. What was in our freezers lasted two days in the biggest block party our neighborhood had ever known. After that we would subsist on canned food and dry goods. Those of us who live in hurricane alley always keep an emergency cache of water and sustenance, enough for at least two weeks. Our hoarded toilet paper was enough to last for months. We weren't worried.

Moreover, as the kids who had been returned to us explained, the indigenous people who had lived in these lands before us had had no supermarkets, no convenience stores, no enormous trucks burning petrol as they spread their exhaust from one corner of the nation to the other, just to bring them their food. They who had settled on the very land where we lived today had had no power-hungry ovens, dishwashers or A/C units. Yet they survived, for millennia.

Luna returned to us with all sorts of practical knowledge. She was amazed at discovering hundreds of useful survival tactics while the children were in the Everglades. The fairies had been patient and thorough teachers and taught them how to use the bounty of nature for survival.

There were all sorts of edible plants around us. It was an art knowing which ones were edible, which ones were harmful. Even though the fairies didn't eat plants, except for the pollen of flowers, they remembered this knowledge of the indigenous people who had lived here before us, the very ones our European descendants chased away or killed off instead of learning from them.

When the children were held in the Everglades, they learned to gather the fruits of wild blackberries, blueberries, mulberries, beautyberries, seagrapes and muscadine grapes; to make salads with purslane, dandelion, spiderwort and chicory (this last plant also has roots that can be roasted, ground and brewed into substitute coffee); to dig up the roots of betony, known as wild radishes, and those of the taro root, a type of colocasia, similar to my elephant ear! Additionally, there were those exotic plants that had escaped cultivation and spread far and wide that were edible, like pink sorrel, Malabar spinach, Red Shield hibiscus, and the tubers of the sword fern. The children were taught to use twigs from the Indian rosewood tree as toothbrushes. Then, for snacks, there were roasted acorns. Who knew that humans could eat the acorns of our local oak tree, the Southern live oak, *Quercus sempervirens*? Sure, the natural tannin found in them made them very bitter, but all one had to do was throw the acorns into a tub of hot water three or four times in order to leach the tannin out of them. Those of us who drink red wine realize that a little tannin never hurt anyone.

Once this useful knowledge became part of our new way of living, we wondered why we had lived for so long expecting—and demanding—that our spinach and snow peas be transported from California, our pineapples from Hawaii, our grapes from Chile. We could grow so much in our own back yards. For those not horticulturally inclined, buying locally grown food at the supermarkets became a necessity, but not a hardship.

Just weeks after the fossil fuel culprits had been removed from power, along with many of their politician cronies, the renewable sources faction was able to turn the lights back on, with the important difference that using the remnants of fossil fuels would be temporary. Extraction, of course, was halted immediately. The gas, coal and oil that was already in the system would be used up as the renewables were speedily brought up to production and linked to the electrical grid. All funds that originally had been used by and for the fossil fuel industry were diverted to the construction and installation of additional renewable-source power plants. It would take time to implement all of our projects but we knew we would be successful longrun.

Quelling the social unrest caused by the dismantling of the fossil fuel industries was also going to take time. Millions of people worldwide were suddenly out of work. Hundreds of thousands had heavy financial losses. But the enviros among us who were also experts in business and industry came up with the groundwork to help them. It wasn't that the rancor we all felt towards the Death Economy folks was all gone. The true reason was that they would be needed in the new Life Economy. The renewables opened up millions of new jobs around the world. What was it to an employee to be engaged in work dealing with the extraction of coal or the refining of petroleum and instead support his family fabricating solar panels or maintaining wind turbines? Now that the renewables were no longer fringe elements of energy production, many employees would be necessary to run them. The financial people also came up with a scheme to assuage the rage of all those ordinary people who had held stocks in the fossil fuel industries. Their losses would be redeemed by stocks in the developing renewable source industries, not at 100% or even 50%, but we all had to make sacrifices. From now on we had to rely on a new way of viewing our human existence on earth, a new mentality that acknowledged our previous destructive ways and demanded its rectification. Deforestation was also on our agenda, as was extraction of metals, overfishing, the proliferation of plastic, and human destruction of animal habitats. We had to convince the whole world that human life was worth preserving, and cleaning up our planet and protecting its other residents were necessary corollaries.

Humans, with a monumental push from the fairies, had managed to overturn a colossal and thoroughly entrenched behemoth: fossil fuels. We knew this was only a start, but a very good one, and we felt we had the impetus to continue the work ahead of us. It would definitely be a long slog, but hope brimmed in our hearts and enthusiasm in our souls. Now that we had won a first battle, and one of the most difficult, we knew we would be able to prevail.[4]

4 The last task that our colloquies executed was to plan for any possible backlash from the fossil fuel people. Bad habits die hard. We came up with six steps to keep this from happening. They are to be found in Appendix D.

Forty-ninth event:

SATURDAY, MAY 30TH

It has been a month since the start of the environmental colloquies. Our lives are getting a bit back to normal. Humans and fairies alike are learning to cope with one another, learning the new rules of open coexistence and coordinated activities. No matter what individual humans thought of the fairies, no one could deny that they were sincerely altruistic. The fairies, of course, no surprise to them, still had to deal with human duplicity and injury. There were humans who distrusted the fairies, who abhorred them for meddling in human affairs, who called them evil and diabolical and refused to have them around. The fairies complied and did nothing to assist them.

The hardcore religious had the most problems accepting the fairies, either their very existence or their beneficence. The bible-thumpers especially vilified the fairies. Many of them, after everything that had happened, still called the fairies a hoax, a way for the liberal tree-hugging granola-munchers to get their way and foist their crackpot political and economical agenda on the rest of society. Those who saw the fairies flitting about called them annoying varmints, insect pests, a scourge, and a new biblical plague. They brought out their insect repellent sprays and dared the vermin to fly past them. That these "pests" were smart enough to stay away from such humans made no impression on them. The true faithful who had no trouble believing in purely imaginary beings and in tenuous tenets could not believe that the very visible—and for some, touchable—fairies were real. These fanciful people had been taught to believe by their ecclesiastic antecedents that they were the master species and overlords of all creation; they continued to think of fairies as dumb critters.

But they weren't the only wackos. When the internet was back, one of the new online conspiracy theories to greet us was that fairies were artificial robots created by an alien race eons ago and released onto the earth as an experiment. The aliens were long gone but the fairies remained and they evolved, from sentinels who kept an eye on the place to creatures who mimicked human culture and society. That they learned to propagate their own kind was a testament to the intelligence of the extraterrestrials who made them.

In the more rational realm, laws were quickly enacted in most nations to protect the fairies. Fairies were defined as intelligent and sentient beings fully deserving of all the laws of safekeeping that protected humans. Sadly, since there were many humans who still could not accept that all humans were worthy of societal safekeeping, these decrees did nothing to quell their desire to murder any fairy they encountered. If only the sacred word of their god had mentioned the existence of fairies there could have been some hope that the ultra-religious could have accepted their existence on the planet. But these people had never even accepted the Darwinian revelations of the 19th century. Against such an entrenched and obdurate mindset, there was nothing that could be done.

But those of us who accepted and appreciated the fairies were having the time of our lives. We were no longer alone. We were ecstatic to know we had a partner sharing our planet, an equal partner with a completely different set of philosophical, ethical and cultural values that were proving to be beneficial to human societies all over the world. Each of us could choose and profit from what the fairies had to offer.

Joan-Agnes, for example, was thick in the learning of Fairyspeak. Even though there were fairy speech sounds impossible for humans to produce, since we lack a syrinx, there were equivalents that were acceptable and perfectly understandable to the fairies. For instance, the sound that the fairies made that sounded like a fingernail running down the teeth of a comb could be substituted by the trilling of the human tongue against the base of the upper teeth, similar to a Spanish double 'r', with an accompanying descending, or ascending, change in pitch by the larynx. Linguists all over the world found that by learning Fairyspeak they could also gather insights into the communication of birds. Linguists and ornithologists united their ranks to establish a new science, ornitholinguistics.

The University of Miami recalled Joan-Agnes from her retirement to spearhead a new addition to their Department of Modern Languages: Fairyspeak. Esperanto, which all fairies learn as a second, third, or fourth language, also returned to the rosters of academia. The new curriculum, which began that fall, was an immediate hit. Students flocked to the new courses. The popularity of two universal languages, Esperanto and Fairyspeak, in high schools and universities across the planet, bode well for the unification of humanity and for its alliance with the fairies and with other species. Had an antidote to the Tower of Babel finally been found?

The science department also had a new entry into the curriculum: Fayology (the Brits opted for Faeology, the French for féeologie, and the Spanish for hadología), either as a separate course or as a blended study with anthropology. Jim was hired by the University to develop it.

The political ramifications of the new anthropo-fairy alliance was as varied as there are nations in the world. In the United States, the president, who had never yielded his bellicose stance against the fairies, was discredited and shunned by the Democrats and even by members of his own party. This was the first time in U.S. history that a president has been labeled a lame duck during his first term, way before the elections. It was said that the president-in-name-only walked the empty halls of the White House bemoaning his undeserved fate, lashing out at his enemies, weeping about his abandonment by all.

Elsewhere in the world, there were ramifications nobody could have predicted. In France, a fairy was named Minister of Agriculture. In neighboring Switzerland, a fairy was elected as one of the seven members of the Federal Council of the Confederation. In Costa Rica, a fairy became head of the National Parks and Reserves. She immediately established corridors between the largest parks to reverse the isolation and fragmentation of animal habitats. UNESCO honored her action by declaring more of the protected areas to be World Heritage Sites.

Likewise in the quotidian life of humans and fairies, fairies began to be incorporated into more pedestrian occupations. Such was the high esteem that people held the fairies for the way they had taken care of the children, that many were asked to manage kid's nursery schools, after-school activities, and extra-curricular learning. The fairies excelled at teaching the kids about nature, the environment, and animal habitats. The medical field hired fairies by the droves, especially in their pharmaceutical research facilities. The plethora of new drugs that resulted from the fairies' vast knowledge of plants was phenomenal.

In restaurants, fairies introduced all sorts of new aromatic spices and plants to all sorts of national cuisines, Asian, Latin, even French and Italian. Why be limited to herbes de Provence? Why not herbes de Patagonie, herbes d'Amazonie, herbes de Zimbabwe? A riot of novel tastes invaded kitchens and new edible fruits and vegetables were added to menus everywhere.

Zip lines and bungee jumping and even theme parks were just about abandoned by the hordes who now sprinted to fairy flight centers. For those with an adventurous spirit, roller coasters and pendulum swings no longer offered enough of a thrill; it was preferable to be taken up into the air by the fairies. On a more serious side, since there still were no electric ambulances, the fairies would take patients to hospitals. They were a much faster transport.

There was another huge benefit to humans who employed fairies in their multifarious activities: fairies were not interested in money and thus asked for no salary. This was a surprise to those who believed in leprechauns and in their pots of gold. But fairies had no use for money; it held no lure and possessed no value. To them a bowl of honey was more of an attractant than a basketful of bank notes.

More recently there was a trend that was spotted first in India and quickly jumped to all nations, especially with teenage FoFs. Girls and boys wore fairies as jewelry and hair ornaments. The fairies dangled from the kids' ears or hung onto their tresses, changing shapes and colors to suit the kids' activities. The fairies seemed to enjoy close human contact and the ability to observe human behavior from up close. The kids also benefited by the companionship of intelligent beings with whom they could converse like constant friends and who had ready answers to any of their questions. The fairies were indeed better than any smart phone. No smart phone produced up to now could have made sure that the kids didn't get into any trouble.

The sister of a girl whom Luna knew from the university managed to get for herself a crew of fairies who specialized in mimicking snakes. The girl sauntered around looking like Medusa.

Fiftieth event:

THE PRESENT AND THE FUTURE

*B*ack at home, life has slipped into a new phase of normalcy. My garden fairies, Luna and I are flourishing as one big boisterous family. We met the rest of Celesta and Luzitha's girl cousins, Lucinthfia, Luzpklrose, Ka'ërpfellge, Lichtkala, and the twins Boralise and Australise (hatched from an egg with a double yolk), and Quercus and Abiès' boy cousins, Laburno, Pistachklus, Cactaciputh, Bombax, Rutacé'al and Sapinus. We also met another brother of Darragh and Gargora's, Baobabus, newly come from Madagascar, accompanied by his wife, Trochilla. Baobabus, as his name implies, imitates a miniature baobab tree, displaying a thick and bare trunk with a small sombrero of foliage on the very top of his head. Trochilla looked like a tiny hummingbird with green iridescent plumage.

We were told that other fairy family members are on their way from far-away lands. Darragh has been preparing a huge gathering of fairies to celebrate a double marriage, that of Celesta with Quercus, and of Luzitha with Abiès. The young fairy couples are going to get hitched in a fairy ceremony, and we humans are invited to the festivities. We have no idea what to expect. The fairy word used for wedding is *krüpchtla*, which means "soaring together." What a beautiful metaphor, we thought. We imagine that sometime during the ceremony flying will be involved.

In the human world, Joan-Agnes and Jim have finally decided to tie the knot. They've know each other for years, but we suppose that they were inspired by the unions of our favorite fairies. Darragh and Gargora, always generous and hospitable, have invited the human couple to have their wedding at the same time as the fairies'. We're not quite sure what goes on in a fairy wedding ceremony so we're rather nervous and excited about it. Will a cloud of fairies take the human couple up in the air so that they can also start their union together by soaring?

Also in the human world, a rumor has been bandied about that Greta and Xiuhtezcatl are planning to join forces. What an environmental power couple they'll be! Enviros all over the world are overjoyed. We know that each one of them has soared high all by themselves. To what heights will they together be able to soar?

Acknowledgments:

I wish to thank my friends—pixies & sprites all of them—for their succor and solace during the writing of this book. Four of them who are particularly endowed with kindness and encouragement, and splendidly graced with the gifts of patience and empathy, read the manuscript and proffered their critiques and judgments, thereby greatly improving the story. Chérie Clark, Holly Iglesias, Maureen O'Hara, and Marie Zurenda: I love you and thank you with all of my heart. Thank you also to my niece, Roxana Luna Muñoz, the instigatrix of all these fairy shenanigans, for her love and support.

A big thanks to Josefina Bustillo Gómez for chasing me through the elephant-ear leaves to take my photo.

Thanks also to the magic fairydust, the fanciful creativity and the delightful skills brought to this story by the very talented Deb Tremper of Six Penny Graphics and the phenomenal artist McKenzie Bunting, whose illustrations bring my fairies to life. They are also adept at keeping the pesky gremlins at bay.

Appendix A:

List of Philosophers mentioned by Darragh in the Twenty-third Event, together with their important works: (from p. 107)

Lucretius: *De Rerum Natura*; *On the Nature of Things* (c. 60 BCE)

Pliny the Elder: *Naturalis Historia*; *Natural History* (AD 77)

Jean-Jacques Rousseau: *Discours sur l'origine et les fondements de inégalité parmi les hommes*; *Discourse on the Origin and Foundations of Inequalities among Men* (1755)

Henry David Thoreau: *Walden* (1854)

George Perkings Marsh: *Man and Nature* (1864); with a new edition, *The Earth as Modified by Human Action* (1874 & 1885)

Alexander F. Skutch: *Moral Foundations: An Introduction to Ethics* (2006)

Michel Serres: *Le Parasite*; *The Parasite* (1980); *Le Contrat naturel*; *The Natural Contract* (1990); *Biogée*; *Biogea* (2010)

Appendix B:

The complete text of what Darragh had to say about human religion, from page 133:

"Ignorant men built entire edifices, whole constructs, based on pure magic. You call it religion. Religion allows you to justify just about anything you want. Nowhere is there religion in nature; you picked it up out of thin air.

"Birds build nests, termites build mounds, beavers build dams, bees build hives, but nowhere do they build places of worship. Religions come and go and those that go are named mythologies and folklore, but they all arise from the same cause: magical thinking.

"The word 'magic' comes from the Persian 'magi' which comes from the Sumerian 'imga,' meaning deep or profound. Magic is a word applied to a way of thinking, to a mass of ideas which gives rise to a mass of doctrines and to a way of acting. Magic is an operative art, a method of behavior; it comes with a set of rules with which to guide human conduct. Newer generations may dismiss previous systems of magic as primitive beliefs of the ignorant, yet continue to create new systems of magic. Throughout human history, this creative fabrication of alternative systems has remained persistent. Even through modern times, new sects, new denominations, adding or deleting rules and regulations, splinter off from previous groups, provoking conflict, hostilities, bloodshed. Each group, each creed, calls its system the 'true religion' and its adherents the 'true believers.' Those outside are the 'infidels' and the 'heathens.'

"Priests were once shamans, pastors and reverends used to be witch doctors; titles and denominations are of little use: they all, the old cults together with the new sects, share the same mechanism of social product. Societies created distinctions of human activity: some became farmers, some blacksmiths, some priests, with the latter given the responsibilities of a learned profession dealing with the arts of divination. From interpretation of natural events such as earthquakes and floods, to complex constructions of astrology and alchemy, to religions as widely disparate as Buddhism and Catholicism, all rely at their base the undisputable fact of belief in magic. Magic is older than the belief in gods, and it continues to permeate all human societies. Spiritual belief is a construct of magical thinking. Man needs to believe in a creator or creators, in divine intervention, in a programmed destiny, and in everlasting life, so in the lack of such things, he needs to fill the void with their creation.

"It has been suggested that belief in religion was an evolutionary trait that helped the individual survive within his local community. To be a part of a unifying social construct gave protective strength over its members. But that theory deflates when you take into consideration the genocide that has taken place throughout human history as the adherents of one religion annihilated those of another. It may be true that there exists an evolutionary law of the 'survival of the fittest,' but 'the fittest' is not necessarily 'the smartest' but it might well be 'the most violent.' Still, if evolution is set on a planetary scale, by the planet, conflict over religion has been an efficient way to cull the numbers of the planet's biggest threat: humans. Ironically, the bigger the threats and the dangers, the more that people cling to their religion, and therefore to their magical thinking.

"The little girl who tears a daisy apart saying, 'He loves me; he loves me not,' is the same as the priest making a fresh batch of blessed water: they both operate under the conviction of wishful thinking. The Book of the Dead of ancient Egypt, full of magical incantations, potent symbols and miraculous images, is no different than the Torah, the Bible, the Koran, or the Popol Vuh, with their own systems of the supernatural, the divine and the overpowering yearning for the hereafter. Religion has always been the attempt by man to bring his gods under his own control, the overreach to have the gods do his bidding. From that to control over the rest of society is but a small step. How to dominate huge swaths of the population so that the priestly class retains its power? They must convince the populace that they must do so and so, pray like this or like that, and strictly follow a myriad of other arbitrary and whimsical canons in order to remain in the gods' good graces. On such principles of crowd management are religions built. The priests succeed in controlling their societies down to the simplest acts of daily household routine, in the rituals of food preparation, in the taboos of their sexual behavior, in the ceremonies of sending off their dead into the afterlife. Everything else is also ruled by magical systems of belief: disease is caused by evil spirits, drought is caused by a vengeful god, pestilence brought on by sinful people, dreams sent by divinities, disaster precipitated by positions of constellations or moving stars. Magic moved man's fate, so man had to mollify fate, pray to it, sacrifice to it, and believe ardently in its power. Remove that power of faith, remove the importance of fate in the lives of men, and whole societies crumble to the ground.

"On such magical thinking rest the foundations of man's behavior, and the future of the planet hangs on what he will do next.

"How can the rest of us, the other inhabitants of this planet, stand idly by and watch man's meltdown with indifference and inaction? He will take most of us with him to oblivion. We need to do something, and we need to do it now.

"The belief in magic got us to this point. Science—true, unfettered and uncensored science—has made great inroads, but at every advance, magic beats it back. Or at least, the hypocrisy of those controlling the magical thinking beats it back. Those making millions out of fossil fuels will never give up the sacred justification they have been given by their god: *Subdue the earth: have dominion over the fish of the sea and over the fowl of the air and over every living thing that moveth upon the earth!*

"To the ignorant mind, nature may seem magical. In the absence of science to help explain the phenomena of nature, the human imagination will invent whole worlds to fill up the vacuum of man's ignorance. Myth, legend, religion, faith, conviction that imaginary realms exist, abound in all cultures throughout the world. You look up and a vision comes to you, complete with a solitary god, but who is really in three pieces, and angels abound—with their own hierarchy, because in the human worlds, even in their fictitious ones, a few are always more important than the rest. Then you look down and a different vision occurs to your wild imagination: demons and brimstone and eternal damnation, whatever that means. Humans cannot look at the night sky without seeing diagrams and plots and quests. Some of you created stories out of whole cloth, or took historical events and embroidered the most elaborate of enchantments around them. Man's biggest error: anthropomorphism. Since humans are so narcissistic that they cannot even begin the attempt to place themselves in the situation of the other creatures, they have lent to everybody else the feelings, preoccupations, and reactions they themselves feel. Lemmings flee areas of high-population concentration; therefore they must be committing suicide as they leap over cliffs. Sloths move slowly because their diet and metabolism require them to be slow, yet humans decide they are lazy. The mouse is timorous, the eagle fierce, the rooster cocky, the pig filthy and the fox crafty. Wherever do these ideas come from? Have you never seen a mouse stand up to a cat? What audacity and fearlessness it is to see! Perhaps that flash of nerve is enough to surprise and distract the cat, and the plucky mouse frequently escapes. Have you never seen a bird of prey be mobbed by tiny sparrows? The little birds will swipe at and harass the bigger bird, at times even striking it, until the raptor leaves the nesting area. Yet you never come up with statements such as 'ferocious as a sparrow,' or 'fearless as a mouse,' because you do not care to see the other creatures as they are, only as you wish them to be, the easier to deal with them and to explain them away. Your creation of vocabulary to fit your needs tells a big story: vermin, pests, infestations, to say nothing of animal names that represent human foibles and some that also become verbs: this person is an ass, that person is a chicken, the one over there is cowed, this one is dogged, the other one badgers somebody else, another weasels around, or goes on a wild-goose chase, or monkeys around, or apes others, or like an ostrich buries his head in the sand (no ostrich has ever done that!), but nobody sees the elephant in the room: man's selfishness. I mean, how can one turn the miraculous, and difficult, laying of an egg into the meaning of 'ending in failure'? Only if it is a creature who knows nothing about what it is to lay an egg; only if it is a creature who belittles the noble hen who does. The narcissist respects nothing outside of his existence.

"We can no longer wait for humanity to put an end to their crimes against the planet. We must act now."

AGENDA OF THE WORLD MEETINGS ON THE ENVIRONMENT:

The following aspects of environmental damage are all interconnected. Solutions to one problem may bring simultaneous solutions to other problems. (from p. 171)

I. Disrespect of other terrans
    A. Dwindling habitats for other species
    B. Decreased biodiversity
    C. Increased species extinction
        i. Plants
        ii. Animals
    D. Introduction of non-native species
II. Overpopulation of humans
    A. Urban expansion
    B. Agriculture
    C. Deforestation/Unsustainable logging
    D. Unsustainable fishing
    E. Energy
        i. Use of fossil fuels
        ii. Nuclear issues
III. Pollution; Waste production; Release of poisons & toxins
    A. Earth
        i. herbicides
        ii. pesticides
        iii. man-made fertilizers/ increased nitrogen production

      iv.   mining/strip mining

      v.   fracking

  B.   Atmosphere

      i.   Acid rain

      ii.   Ozone layer depletion

  C.   Water

      i.   Ocean acidification

      ii.   Freshwater pollution

      iii.   Depletion of marsh areas

      iv.   Red tide

      v.   Proliferation of plastic

IV.   Climate change

  A.   Melting of polar icecaps & glaciers

  B.   Rising sea levels

V.   Fundraising

Appendix D:

How to impede the fossil fuel industry from creeping back to power: Politicians must be coerced into doing what is right for the planet. Since politicians will always bend to the flow of money, they must be released from the sway of influential fossil fuel promoters. These six steps need to be followed by all nations seeking to redress the wrongs done to the environment by the fossil fuel interests. (from p. 193)

1. Declare campaign contributions from fossil fuel interests and unregulated SuperPac spending illegal;
2. Oust agents working for the government regulatory agencies who once worked for the very businesses they are regulating;
3. Halt all government subsidies handed out to the oil, coal and gas industries;
4. Call the fossil fuel industry by a new name, the Death Economy. As it functions it destroys its own resources and nature itself;
5. Call renewal energy sources the Life Economy, since they are constantly replenished and do less damage to nature;
6. Educate the public on the damage done by the oil, coal and gas industries; Educate the public on the solar, wind, hydro/tidal, biomass and geothermal industries.